# *Strange Circumstances*

Weston Kincade, David Chrisley, & Marshall J. Stephens

Discover other titles by Weston Kincade:

*Invisible Dawn: Book One of the Altered Realities Series*

&

*A Life of Death*

Or check out the Authors' sites:

http://www.marshallmakesmedia.com &

http://www.authorwakincade.blogspot.com

\* \* \* \* \*

**Acknowledgements**

We would like to thank our families, editor Katy Sozaeva, Steven Mays Photography, and Renee at The Cover Counts for their support and assistance with this anthology.

I

# Table of Contents

PART ONE - SHORT STORIES: ...................................................................1

UNDETERMINED FATE .............................................................2
ROOTS ...............................................................................17
FALLING ............................................................................26
UNSEEN .............................................................................43
NIGHT EYES ........................................................................50
FREE DOSTER ......................................................................62
CONSIDERATIONS ................................................................71
SANDMEN ...........................................................................86
DING ..................................................................................93
BOBBLE-HEADS ................................................................108
DEMONIC SUPERVISION .....................................................123
LAUNDROMAT ...................................................................134

PART TWO - FLASH FICTION 3X33S ..................................144

COLD ...............................................................................145
SHROUD ...........................................................................145
FLICKER ...........................................................................146
MATCH .............................................................................146
RECOIL .............................................................................147
TRADITIONS ......................................................................148
FLUSH ..............................................................................148
COG .................................................................................149
COMPANY .........................................................................149
KARMA .............................................................................150
SAINTHOOD .......................................................................150
MAKEOVER ........................................................................151
NIGHT-TERRORS ................................................................151

AUTHOR'S NOTE: ............................................................152

A LIFE OF DEATH .............................................................155

A PARANORMAL COMING-OF-AGE MYSTERY ABOUT ONE BOY'S PAIN AND
HARDSHIP ENDURED IN A SMALL VIRGINIA TOWN. ...................................155

# Part One - Short Stories:

The question of fate goes back beyond written record, and everyone finds themselves considering mortality at times. But few people are actually challenged to discover the extents to which fate and their own desires can take them. How far does your sanity stretch?

These stories are an attempt to open your eyes and minds to the possibilities, however unlikely, that even you might wind up on the long end of a short chain or playing a hand of cards with death, your life hanging in the balance. Explore the unknown in the upcoming stories, and above all, enjoy the ride.

## Undetermined Fate

The darkness parted and my mind whirled back to life. *What happened? Where the hell am I?*

A man's deep, sinuous voice chuckled. "Welcome to Limbo, Travis. Care to make a wager?" His voice was calm but confident, and his tone held experience.

*Wager, what do I have to bet?* In answer to my unspoken question, three octagonal chips glowed blue atop a black, marble table. Faint swirls of gray were embedded in the tabletop and reflected the light, but not far. An inky fog dimmed everything within six inches, and an aching chill seeped through my jeans from the matching bench. Picking up one of the chips, a silver lightning bolt gleamed fiercely across its face.

The sound of fabric sweeping over the polished marble filtered through the air, and an arm extended from the man's direction. His body was a black silhouette in the misty existence, but his visible hand was dark, almost chocolate, with well-manicured fingers. A silver band adorned his thumb, and a stamped hourglass was etched onto the ring's surface. It sprang to life once his hand stopped, and the glass rotated before my eyes. Miniscule grains of silver sand began their journey south. He paused a moment, allowing me to take it all in. Beneath his fingers were three sparkling cards, face down, with scroll work reminiscent of Greek artistry. His hand was mere inches away and revealed a white sleeve that stopped at his forearm. The cloth flowed from him with enough room to encompass a bowling ball, and an identical golden pattern stitched its way around the edge.

When the man withdrew, I slid the cards from the table. They were more like tarot than the playing cards I'd grown accustomed to. Memories flashed before me, revealing the disparity; many nights spent at Atlantic City casinos. The cards depicted pantomiming jesters and glistened in stark contrast to the shadowed world I'd appeared in. One pleaded to me with waving arms as though beckoning me forward. On the second, the jester fled with eyes cast back over his shoulder, while the third was absent of movement. The archaic comedian instead stood with arms crossed and feet spread wide as though exercising. However, his face was set in consternation with eyes that bored into mine. I shuddered, then slid the card's gleaming outline behind the others and looked away.

Something dimly lit the edges of my new world with gray morning rays. Dark shapes were silhouetted at the edge of my murky vision, much like the man who dealt the cards. Shadowed columns were spaced every couple feet around the small area. It was as though we were at the center of an ancient Greek courtyard, but the air held death in its permeating silence. The atmosphere was completed by the dank smell of stagnation. I reached out to touch the moving shapes, but felt nothing more than dense condensation.

"Come on, make a bet," urged a tinny voice to my right. "I ain't got all night."

"Why, you have all the time imaginable, Everett," replied the white-robed man. There was a hint of laughter in his serene voice, as though he knew the punch line to a comedy we were unknowingly acting out. Everett's figure folded his arms with a harrumph.

"I'll bet this," I muttered, trying to find my voice. The mist muffled its vacant echo, as though no walls were near enough for

3

comfort. I slid the chip to the center of the table with feigned confidence.

"That's one favor wagered," added the older man like a lackluster sports announcer. "Passion, yes, you won't need that favor anymore. So what did you do with this Passion? Just one instance from your life?"

*Favor?* I wondered, but the thought was fleeting. *What is this?* My mind jogged through the dark recesses within, but came up empty. I stuttered over something to say before seizing an idea. "Y-y-yes, once, I cared for a –"

"You lie!" The dark man interrupted. "You never cared for anything more than yourself."

My mouth hung wide. He was right. I could barely remember my past, but the certainty of his words was irrefutable. Before I could utter a response, he swept the glowing chit off the table and into a bag. It clattered against others in a growing collection. His silhouetted face turned to a long-haired, slender form to my left and resumed his earlier calm.

"And what will you wager, Lauren?"

A feminine voice with breathy undertones rasped, "What favor do you ask of me?"

*What happened to her?*

I couldn't take my eyes from her slim outline. So far as I could tell, she appeared to be at her peak. She was fit and had a frame that would have put any Bond movie-intro to shame. Something clicked in the back of my mind like a switch.

*A woman much like her sat bound and gagged before me, but in vivid detail; a checkered, blue bandana was tied around her head, holding her mouth open like a horse's bit. It matched the ribbon in her brunette hair. My fingers encircled the soft flesh of her neck. Her eyes widened into pleading orbs. Thick, red blood flowed from where the jugular had been severed and streamed over my fingers.*

*Did I do that?* I couldn't remember, and no answer came. Instead, the smell and sight became strangely alluring… intoxicating even. It was a feeling I could drown in.

"Whichever," the elderly man answered with a wave of his hand, pulling me from the vision. "It won't matter. You will use every favor you've earned in life."

I peered down at my two remaining chips, or favors, as he called them. My heart began beating like a speed-infused bass drum. "Wait! What about me?"

The old man continued as though he hadn't heard. I screamed for him to wait, but he only crooked a finger in my direction. The deathly mist collected around me, obscuring my vision, and absorbed my words.

"Then, here is my Dedication," she whispered and slid a chip infused with a silver swirl across the table.

A low chuckle came from our Dealer then. "You are most certainly dedicated, but perhaps if it were Loyalty instead, you wouldn't be here."

He picked up the favor and flipped it into the air toward his bag. I couldn't take my eyes from the spinning coin; its whirling flight seemed to take an eternity. It expanded in my vision and I closed my eyes to break the link. I opened them onto a scene I couldn't control.

*A young woman's hands diligently copied notes, my eyes (no, it was her eyes) strayed up to the professor. Each time, I could feel a*

5

*blush rising in her cheeks. Her hand had a wedding ring on it, as did his. They didn't match. The scene blurred, and I found myself in an office, my inbox piled high. A man's voice broke in behind me, "You are such a hard worker, but you don't have to be." Something else was added to my inbox, a wrapped condom dropped on the pile. I watched as his broad shoulders and silver hair disappeared into the office at the end of the hall. I picked up the condom and followed.*

The scene changed again, this time to a club.

*It was dark and smoky. Latex-clad servers weaved between groups of customers. I marveled at the number of suits rubbing elbows with the denizens of a world I thought only existed in movies. I didn't particularly like the man whose arm I was holding, but he was the most familiar thing there. I clung to him like a buoy in stormy seas. A girl has to do whatever it takes to get ahead in the corporate world, and while I "worked" late, my husband sat at home spending my paycheck. I loved him, but he lacked ambition. In the back of the club, we were welcomed to a table by a man that looked very familiar, but I couldn't place him. Mid-thirties, broad-shouldered, short but built well. An intense leer beamed from behind clear, blue eyes. He and my boss shook hands, "Travis, it's so good to see you again. I'd like you to meet Lauren."*

The vision faltered. That was me. I began to shake. I wanted to vomit. I didn't remember that, but she did. The coin finished its slow arc and joined the others.

"Are you all right, Travis? It is just a game after all. That is what you always used to tell everyone." The dark man's words twisted in my gut.

"Can we please just get on with this? I have other things to do, and more important people to do them with." Everett's voice was almost pleading. He seemed on the verge of tears. I wondered what he saw as Lauren's dedication took its slow journey through the darkening mist. He was still hard to make out. He looked slender and tall, but his clothing was dark and drew his lines out into the shadows. He slouched in on himself, minimizing what was probably an impressive six-foot-plus height. I studied him, hoping to get some insight into whom he might be. With Lauren I got that image, but with him it just gave me a headache. Or, more accurately, I felt something press into the back of my skull. I reached back to find nothing, but every time I looked at him, the pressure returned. He scared me more than this place, the fog, and the living cards in my hand.

"Of course we can, Everett," The Dealer intoned. "We're waiting on your bet. What will you wager?"

He looked down at his cards and paled a bit more in the dim light. "I have only one favor to bet with, so it must be my Patience."

"Everyone in then?" The Dealer asked. I heard the familiar flip, flip as The Dealer's card came off the deck and onto the table. The Dealer put it down with such force that a puff of air from beneath pushed aside the mist so that its face was clear.

It was a boy sitting on the floor with a top. The look on his face was radiant with delight.

From one side, Everett drew in a breath that even the most rookie poker player would know. It meant that he liked what he saw. No sound came from Lauren, no hint of her take on the situation.

"Choose," The Dealer said.

"How does this work?" I asked. "What are the rules?"

7

The Dealer said, "That's not how it works here. You have to learn as you go. But don't worry just yet. It is Everett's turn. Watch and learn for once, Travis."

My cheeks burned like they did in Catholic school.

*Catholic School. I went to Catholic school!* Joy came with the memory, joy at the fact that I remembered something, anything. It faded as soon as I realized that it helped me not one bit.

Everett threw down a card from the two in front of him with a snort of contempt. Lauren did the same, though she had three cards, the same as I did. I lifted up mine and guessed. I chose the one looking over his shoulder. It felt like the cautious bet.

As I pushed it forward, I felt it stick to the table like it had been put there with superglue.

The dealer passed his hands over the cards we played. The table vibrated, and I felt like I was at the top of a roller coaster.

"Now," The Dealer said. "We reveal."

The cards flipped over without anyone touching them, slamming onto the table like a gavel on the judge's bench.

Everett said, "Gotcha."

I looked at his card and found it was a figure with beckoning arms, like mine, except where I had a jester, Everett's card bore a king in a tarnished crown and tattered robes.

The dealer said, "The Future against Joy?"

"I'll be happy to get out of here, won't I?" asked Everett.

The Dealer said, "Maybe so. Maybe not. No matter. You win."

Everett sat back. I could feel the smugness rolling off of him. Maybe a lucky streak was what made the damn mist around us.

"Now you, Travis."

"Failure," The Dealer said flatly. "You have no innocent Joy in your past."

"What?" I said in confusion. Before the word was past my lips, I felt the bottom drop out from under me.

*Another dream. I was in the back of a car... no, a limousine. The taste of high-quality gin was on my lips. Someone leaned up against me, and we laughed, nearly spilling our drinks. It was a woman with a familiar, unforgettable figure, and she was drinking champagne. I knew it was her third, and the first two went down in under three minutes.*

*Her weight against my arm was a welcome thing. I could see down her blouse, but not enough. We weren't alone, but I paid little attention to the other person in the compartment. I wanted this woman like a schoolboy wants ice cream. And for some reason, I knew I'd likely have her.*

"Another round," someone said. The there and here mixed and I didn't know if they were talking about the game or booze. I wanted to go back to the scene in the car. I wanted to feel like she was making me feel. I wanted simply to want something that much again.

But I couldn't. The knowledge filled me from the front of my skull to my gut. I might never feel that again if I didn't win this damn game.

I felt the bench under me and looked around the table, still unable to make out anything clearly that wasn't the cards. I felt hollow.

I looked over at Lauren's card. It was the past. I hadn't heard whether that meant she won or lost.

The Dealer held up something, and the mists parted so I could see it. It was a die. There were images on the side of it in place of the dots, and as he rolled it across his fingertips, I could see that there were hexagons, rectangles, and two other figures that I couldn't make out.

"The roll," he said and let the die fall to the table.

Octagon.

"Winners receive a Favor," The Dealer said. "Losers forfeit an additional Favor."

The cards we had played all went up in little flashes of blue flame. I heard Everett chuckle, a cruel and malicious sound.

"The past?" he said. "Dumbass. You can't win back the past."

I was seriously starting to hate that guy.

I looked down and saw that my chips had been reduced to one chip. I started to ask The Dealer, "What gives?" but he already had something to say. "You lost Independence. My choice. They weren't doing you much good anyway."

I felt cold to my toes.

"Don't worry, Travis," The Dealer said. "You've got one more Favor: Cruelty. It's done you well in the past, hasn't it?"

I said, "Cruelty is a favor?"

"For a priest, no. For a butcher, yes," the old man's voice intoned. "You were no priest. Now, place your bets. This next round could be important for you."

I bit my tongue and slid my last chip forward.

Everett said, "Let's go with Cunning this time." He flipped the chip he'd won last round at The Dealer. I looked at it, trying to peer into it intentionally this time. It worked.

10

*I watched as a woman made out with me on a couch. It was the woman from the car, I knew. She was even more tipsy, and viewing the scene in the third person, I wanted her as myself and as the man whose eyes I was borrowing. But as the latter of the two, I knew she was doing a job. She was the bait, the kind a high roller would go for, window dressing for a game with the highest of stakes.*

*My eyes looked toward me and said, "So how long till your girl shows up with the other boys?"*

*I heard Everett's voice lie, saying, "About an hour. You've got time. Let me give you kids some space."*

*I sneered, left the room, and waited for the girl to slip a mickey into the other Travis's drink.*

I was back at the card table as soon as the doors closed. The transition was instantaneous, and it was Lauren's turn to bet.

The Dealer asked, "What'll it be?"

"Remorse," Lauren replied.

She looked down at her chips; she had five left. I didn't know if that was good or bad for me. The only thing I could do was play the game.

The Dealer flipped his card. This time it revealed a man on one knee accepting a crown on his head, his eyes downcast.

I looked at my cards. The still one felt wrong. If over-the-shoulder was the Past and the other moving one was the future, then the still one was probably the Present. And my Present right then didn't feel much like I was being crowned. I played the Future.

Everett smacked down the present. Lauren played the Future, her card like mine but with an innocent maiden in place of the jester. The table's faint light illuminated her hands as she played the card,

11

slender and graceful like the rest of her. It didn't take a photographic memory to tell me it was the same Lauren I'd been with on the couch, the one who tried to drug me.

The details were coming back like a dream that I didn't want to remember.

The Dealer said to Everett, "You fail."

"But I'm winning!" he said.

"No," The Dealer said. "You're not. You've never accepted anything with Humility."

I looked over at Everett. The mist seemed to part before his fear. His eyes widened with panic. But he was searching for a way to win.

The Dealer ignored him and said, "Travis, you win a hand. You too, Lauren. Well done. And now... the die."

I watched it tumble onto the table and clatter to a conclusion. Octagon.

"A Favor again," The Dealer said. "That means you're out, Everett."

Everett paled, as though the mists wanted us to see the failure. Then he was gone, drawn back into the shadows before he could scream. If I'd blinked, I'd have missed it.

I looked down at my chips. I was back to a set of three. She had six. We both had one card left, the Present.

"Place your bets," The Dealer said.

I said, "Passion."

Lauren rasped, "Regret, one more time."

The Dealer asked her, "Haven't you had enough?"

Lauren leaned forward. The light cast long shadows across her face, revealing beauty and contempt. She snapped, "Just deal."

The Dealer replied, "So be it."

Lauren slid the chip over. In it, I again saw things as they once were.

At least this time I was an earlier version of myself. *I sniffed the gin and tonic in my hand, then looked back at the door the men disappeared through. Lauren's pulse quickened under my hand. She'd botched it. I shook my head and lunged forward. The struggle was brief, and soon I had Lauren's wrists tied to the chair.*

*I moaned and grunted as I bound and gagged her body, making a good show of it. Anyone waiting to rob me at the door would be convinced that all they'd have to do is wait for the afterglow, and I'd be easy pickins.*

*Lauren screamed against the gag when I pulled the nickel-plated revolver from the holster on my ankle. She fought against the phone cord binding her wrists, her eyes following me as I hid. I screamed, "Oh god, oh god," as though I were close to the end and it was about to be someone's payday.*

*Everett burst in, gun drawn. When he saw Lauren tied up, he stopped and looked to his side, where I stood with my pistol leveled, less than ten feet away. But it was too late.*

*Lauren's wrists slipped free. She jumped in the middle, her cry of "Wait!" swallowed by a pair of gunshots. One sped over her shoulder and caught me in the chest as Everett maneuvered to use her as a shield. The other punched through Lauren's belly, out the back, and into Everett's side.*

I opened my eyes.

"There's not room for all three of you tonight," The Dealer said. "Do you understand the stakes now?"

"Oh yeah. I get it."

"Then let's play," The Dealer continued.

His card was a man standing on a cliff, raising a fist to the world and screaming. I threw down my card. Lauren did likewise.

"Defiance," The Dealer said. "The Present certainly holds that for both of you."

The die came up on a rectangle this time. "You get back a card. Choose, the Past or the Future?"

"I didn't think you could get the Past back," I interrupted.

"Everett said that," The Dealer replied. "Was he ever running the game, though?"

"I guess not. I'll take it." I looked at Lauren, enjoying the game at last. The mist had parted, and I could see her clearly now. Her face was stained with tears. She had five chips again to my two. And she didn't look happy to be ahead.

She mumbled, "I'll take the Future."

"All right," The Dealer said. The cards appeared. "Bets?"

My gaze lingered on Lauren. Her horror and anguish flowed off her in waves. It was like I was still in her head. Her husband would never remember her as they met, only as she was found. Her last act was to protect a man who disgusted her, but who she didn't think should die.

The fun of the game seemed to plummet through an invisible hole, leaving the room cold and desolate.

Turning to The Dealer, I said, "Let's make this interesting. Winner take all."

"Should she agree…?" The Dealer responded, as though the idea were certainly an interesting one.

"I agree," Lauren interjected. "Let's get this over with. I'm tired of playing your game."

"So be it," The Dealer said. The tumblers to a lock I couldn't see fell into place.

The card came up with a picture of a newborn. Life.

Lauren started to cry.

The Dealer looked at me and said, "So… the past."

I said, "Yeah."

"In order for her to win, you have to lose. You can't both win."

"I know," I muttered solemnly.

"So," he said. "Do you understand the rules now?"

"Yeah," I answered.

"And did you win?" he asked.

"No."

"What?" Lauren shouted. "What does that mean?"

"It means I forgive you." My chips slid across the table, merging with hers. My remaining card disappeared in a puff of smoke. The eight chips came together in a ring. The Dealer reached out and took it, then threw it between us. It hung in the air for a moment and stretched to become a door.

I looked at Lauren, her face confused but the spark of hope back in her eyes. "Go. I'll settle up here. Good game."

She stood and said, "I'm sorry."

"I know. Go," I continued, ushering her toward the door.

She stepped through and away the door went.

It was just me and The Dealer now. He regarded his ring. Only a few grains remained in the upper part of the hourglass.

"So you lost," he said. "You agreed that life was in her future, not yours."

"I did."

"One problem," The Dealer replied. "To lose means you had to be wrong."

"Is that how it works?"

"Yes." The table cracked. His ring cracked. Suddenly, it was like I was falling, the columns and marble table flew past, the room spun, and air whooshed past my ears. Then, I gasped as someone yelled, "Clear!"

Tubes streamed out of my nose and arms. When I pried my eyes open, I glimpsed them wheeling Lauren out on a stretcher. She looked back at me before disappearing through the door. A paramedic was zipping Everett's body up in a black body bag.

*I wasn't sure what fate had in store for me from here on. But I was certain of one thing. I'd just broken even.*

## **Roots**

The train car shuddered and the wheels squealed, interrupting Adrianna as she pecked at her laptop keyboard. The great beast trundling over the rails couldn't stop on a dime, and she watched as the moonlit trees outside her window slowed. Groans escaped the mouths of the occupants around her, and a frizzy-haired woman in front of Adrianna panicked, twisting in her seat in an effort to match the chaos nested on her head.

"Wha-what was that?" the woman stammered searching the passenger car for the demon that had to be descending on them.

Adrianna sighed. "Just the brakes. I'm sure it's nothin'."

But was it? Trains didn't stop like that for raccoons or even cows: at least not that she knew of. A calm, bass voice echoed from the speakers overhead. "Passengers of train 30, we've made an emergency stop, but there is nothing to fear. We will soon be back on course. Again, I apologize for our earlier two-hour delay. At this time, it doesn't appear that we will be any later, but we'll keep you posted. Please return to your seats and get some rest."

The speaker clicked off, and muttering instantly flooded the passenger car. The attempt to assuage their fears had piqued Adrianna's curiosity, and it seemed she wasn't alone. Before long, most of the train's occupants resumed their earlier tasks: pecking at mp3-players and computers, resting, or reading books and e-readers. They were too engrossed in their own lives to let the temporary delay distract them. The frazzled woman was the only other occupant that seemed even mildly concerned.

"What do you think happened?" she whispered, peering through the headrests in front of Adrianna. "Do you think it's terrorists?"

"Oh, God! Get real, lady," snapped a young man in khaki shorts and a T-shirt after removing his earbuds. Adrianna hadn't heard him say a word since they left, but now she wished he'd kept his mouth shut. "Look," he continued, "we aren't even in Toledo anymore. We're out in God's country now, where the mountain folk'll introduce themselves by saying, 'You gotta purdy mouth'. Terrorists would run screaming if they saw this place. There's no way this is an attack." He snubbed the frantic woman with an upraised nose and put his earbuds back in, refusing to look anywhere but out the window.

The woman's hair shook as she huddled into her seat.

*Thanks for nothin'!* Adrianna wanted to scream. *Can't you tell she's scared?* He wouldn't have heard anyway, with the drum and guitar solos screaming so loudly she could discern the band from two seats away. *ZZ Top... even jerks can have good taste.* She'd been thankful that no one had booked the seat between them, but now she was having second thoughts. Anyone would've been better than the sobbing woman and this insolent prick. She had to get out of there. Adrianna slapped her laptop shut and rose.

"Ma'am, please take your seat," warned a uniformed woman from the end of the train car.

Adrianna glanced back at the two seated around her and the bald man with the squared jaw sitting next to the frantic woman. He seemed to be the only one in their section also attempting escape, but rather into a magazine held mere inches from his face. Her mind raced, searching for an excuse. "I-I have to go to the bathroom. I can't wait."

Before the train employee could say more, Adrianna dashed past and into the next florescent-lit car. It was much the same as hers, and she continued down the aisle past kids, college students like herself, and people waiting to return to their lives. The next one was the same, but as she reached the last passenger car, the door opened into darkness blacker than the world outside. The chatter of people died as the door sealed behind her. No moon shone through the car windows… in fact, there seemed to be none in the closed room. But as her eyes adjusted, a subtle, jagged line of green glowed in the center of the room, trekking up to eye level.

*What in the world?* Adrianna stepped closer. Something crunched beneath her tennis shoe and she looked for the source, but the bare scar of light didn't reach her feet. Taking a deep breath, she neared the glow, suppressing her imagination at each crunch underfoot. As she approached, the light cast an eerie glow on the floor of the car, but what she found made no sense. Dead leaves and twigs littered the ground as though she'd stepped deep into the heart of a forest.

*That's not supposed to be here.* Her eyes returned to the base of the light. It was coming from something. Kneeling down, she ran a hand over the enormous roots running between her feet. The scar of glowing light was seeping from inside a huge tree. Her hand and eyes climbed the rough texture until they came upon a slick surface, slightly curved. Adrianna looked closer, but leaped back as the outline of a fireman's helmet was illuminated by the growing glow. The gruesome scar branched and grew at her touch, defining the curves of a man's face below the helmet. His body and uniform were encased in the tree as though it had grown around him. Adrianna touched his cheek with gentle fingers. The breath she'd been holding hissed past her lips. His skin was cold, but still tender. At the front of his burnished, red helmet stood a large number seven, bordered by the words 'Insurance' and 'FDNY' above and below.

*Where did this come from, and how did the tree grow around him so quickly?*

Before she could voice the question, a queer voice croaked from the other side of the tree, "That man's been here for the last hundred years, but you, my dear, are new."

Adrianna's head swiveled left and right like the frazzled woman's had earlier, but in this darkness there was nothing to see beyond the outlined man and leafless tree. "Where am I? How'd I get here?"

"Here?" repeated the guttural voice. "You're still on train 30, the express from Toledo to DC."

"But… it can't be. Did you stop the train?"

"Stop… start, the train's movement means nothing to us."

"Us?" asked Adrianna.

"Yes," a croaking voice behind her said. Adrianna felt a puff of cold breath on the back of her neck with each word. "We are many. Legion. We live in the space between breaths and on the side of the door you cannot see. We vacation in your nightmares and fill our pantry with the thoughts that you had just a second ago, but then blink and forget."

"Stop," the voice from the impossible tree said. "We need not offer our full honorifics here, my brother. Be more kind to our guest."

A wicked and menacing chuckle came from the one behind her. "As you wish."

Adrianna felt her feet lift and warm furs curve around her legs and back, a chair made of some living and breathing thing supporting her in space. She could feel it rise and fall, feel a heartbeat against her back.

The second voice was circling her now. Adrianna could see him move, though couldn't make out the details of his form. She asked, "Is there something I can do for you? Because if not, I'd really like to stop having this acid trip and get back to my seat."

Dozens of tiny voices tittered and jeered in the darkness. It became very hard to control her breathing.

"Your mind is your own," the first voice said. "You're just not asking the right questions."

"What questions do I need to ask?" Adrianna replied.

"We cannot tell you."

"Then why did you bring me here?"

"Ah," the second voice said. "She found one. Took her long enough."

The voice behind the tree interjected, "That's enough of that. Now, girl, what makes you assume we brought you here? You were the one who walked and you were the one who arrived. Why do you think you did not choose your own course?"

"Because…" she began. But she realized she didn't have any follow up to that.

"Dark," the second voice said. "Rich."

"What?" Adrianna asked. She'd lost track of him, though his footfalls were heavy. Her eyes had begun to adjust to the pitch darkness. More shapes were appearing in the tree. There was a man in a suit higher in the limbs; she had mistaken his outstretched arms for branches. Just above him was a woman, her hair now like straw, shaking gently.

"Your name," the second one said, "Adrianna. That's what it means."

"Good to know," she muttered. She was ashamed at how frightened it sounded. "Who the hell are you?"

"And another," the voice from behind the tree said. "We're teachers, merchants that deal in wisdom, present among many cultures in many times."

"Sounds good." A nervous smile came to her lips.

The second one asked, "Really? Wisdom comes at a price. That's why so few have it, you know. We don't give it away for free."

"Is that why I'm here?" Adrianna was trying not to let the fear crack in her voice. This would all make sense soon, she was sure of it. "You're going to teach me some of this terrible wisdom?"

"And at last," the first voice, the voice in the tree, said. "You've asked the best question. You're here because you wanted to be. And we will teach you, but only time will tell if it's wisdom."

"I… I didn't want to come here," Adrianna protested.

There was a hand on either side of her living seat. She could see the sharp nails at the ends of the furry fingers. Heavy breaths tickled her ear; puffs of air that she was sure were making their way past sharp fangs.

The second one hissed, "Yes, you did. We do that which we wish, even when we don't think we have a choice. A man jumping out of a burning building might not want to fall and go splat, but he wants to avoid burning more. And you soon will have a choice."

"Did they get a choice?" she asked, pointing at the tree.

"They did," the voice in the tree replied. "The same as you now have."

"This tree is 'THE' tree of legend. You Christians call it the Tree of Knowledge. The Norse called it Yggdrasil. It is Samoyed and axis mundi. And we are the Greeks' Kallikantzaroi, though we tend the tree, not saw at it the way we were portrayed in those times." The hissing voice stopped for a moment. After a long breath that seemed to stretch for days, he continued. "Every so often, someone is born in possession of something the Tree is missing. We watch them grow. If that thing is still a part of them by the time they are mature enough for the choice, we find them. In you is something rich and dark to be added to the Tree."

The first voice interjected, "The choice is… do you add yourself to the Tree and help guide humanity in its cosmic journey? Or, do you deny us and wake up in your train seat believing what you will of this encounter?"

"A life forever in the Tree or my life…" Adrianna mused. "There is always another choice. I am familiar with these stories. There must be a way to guide humanity, add to the Tree, and still live my life."

"In all these centuries, you are the first to ask. You can challenge me for a seed." The owner of the second hissing voice dropped from the branches to bow before her. A small, gnarled creature, he looked as though he were half sculpted from lumps of mismatched clay. "If you win, you remember everything and get a seed to plant near your heart so that it may guide you, and you may teach it. If you lose, you become part of the Tree. Not as they are, but buried in the roots so that your strength of will can nourish the Tree as your soul adds to its purpose."

"Has no one before gotten a seed?"

"There have been those that were so bright at birth that they were given a seed. They were visionaries, the best at what they chose to do." Voice one's tone changed and became melancholy. "It has been many generations since we have found a child worthy of one."

"What is the challenge?"

"You said you know the stories. The test is always a riddle challenge. And by rule, the challengee begins. What falls without breaking and breaks without falling?" There was a crooked smirk on the goblin's face as he let fly with the first riddle.

"Night and Day. But I didn't accept," Adrianna protested.

Voice one whispered, "You didn't have to. You laid the challenge."

"Alright. How many sides does a circle have?"

"Two. Inside and outside. Name three consecutive days without using the words Sunday, Monday, Tuesday, Wednesday, Thursday, Friday, or Saturday."

"Yesterday, Today, and Tomorrow. How many months have 28 days?"

"All of them. How far can a man walk into the woods?" The smirk became a full-fledged smile on the imp's face.

"Halfway, the other half he's walking out. A mother has seven children, half of them are boys. How is this possible?"

"They are all boys. Think of words ending in –gry. In the English language there are three of them. 'Angry' and 'Hungry' are two. What is the third word?" He straightened up, eyes glowing with obvious confidence in his superiority.

Adrianna shook her head. "You told it wrong. Most people do. The way you told it has no answer, as there are five words in English that end in –gry. It's just that three of them aren't used anymore. The riddle is supposed to go… Think of words that end in –gry. 'Angry' and 'Hungry' are two of them. In the English language there are three words. What's the third?"

Voice quivering, the little man replied, "That one has no answer either. We will throw them both out."

"But mine has an answer, 'Language'. The rest of it is misdirection. The riddle is 'In the English language there are three words. What is the third?' The: one. English: two. Language: three."

The creature stopped, bowed, and held out a seed. "Plant it well."

"I will." Adrianna tipped back her head and swallowed the seed. On the way back to her seat, the train started again. New hope for the day took root in her breast along with a small sapling of the 'Tree'.

## Falling

There's a sharp ping of metal snapping, and then John's stomach lurches into his throat. If that isn't enough to tell him he is falling, the roar of wind rushing past his ears confirms it. That most deafening of white noises is impossible to disguise if you've ever been skydiving. The falling isn't John's issue. He can't see. He's certain there is no blindfold, and there isn't the pain he would associate with losing his eyes. So, what did she do to him?

John's been falling a very long time… an impossibly long time. HALO jumps don't take hours. Falling doesn't leave time for reflection. He has time for reflection. Who is he, really? How did he get here? How does he get out? Something about the first question frightens him. Not ready for that sort of introspection, John moves to the second.

The badge said Ian Masters, as did the smooth, looping signature in the log book. The security was tight, but he was well prepared. His lockpicks were Kevlar; his boot knife was ceramic. His smart-phone was far smarter than any agency would anticipate. His team was good. They had buried a code breaker and a satellite uplink in his phone; that way even if he couldn't get out, the information could. Industrial espionage is a very profitable career, and he had exceeded the life-expectancy of a spy by at least a decade. This would be his last job. Never mind that he had said that after the last three. The silver creeping in at his temples and the amount of time needed for recovery after the last job convinced him that it was time to retire.

John shakes his head. *That's not relevant.* What happened after he got past security?

Ian was early for his meeting and was left to wait in the public areas of the Dawbry Corp tower. The large, open area was littered with propaganda and awards meant to breed goodwill in visitors regardless of what had led them there. The news had been harping on unproven claims that Dawbry was poisoning the land, causing hideous mutations. Families were clogging the phone lines looking for spouses and fathers that went to work one day and never came home. The agency wanted an inside view of the tower, and Ian was the best; good enough to know that in the age of computers, the skeletons in the closet were easiest found at the servers, not the offices. The servers had incredible net-based security. One of the agency hackers was sent to a psych-ward after trying to crack it. But the physical security was usually very lax. The alarm on the fire door was easy to disable. The lock on the basement was complex, but Ian was better. There wasn't any human security down there, and to his surprise, Ian didn't see any automated security either. He found an access point to the server and connected his phone. It would take some time, so he decided to look around. Near the back of the basement was something putrid. It smelled like a mixture of a slaughterhouse and a sewer. The source of the stench was a large tube coming from the back of one of the servers and going into the floor.

*Click.* No time for further investigation, someone was there. A sultry woman's voice called out, "It's time for your meeting, Mr. Masters."

The panic came instantly. Ian locked it down as fast. How could she know he was in this room? No one had seen him. There'd been no cameras.

Wait... he'd *seen* no cameras. None were on the layout he'd gotten from his contact. None of that meant they weren't there. *Stupid, old man.*

"My employer is eager to meet you," said the woman, "but he won't tolerate any dawdling. Leave your phone and let it do whatever it needs to. You can get it on your way out."

Ian ran through the possibilities. If this was a bluff, there would be security. He'd hear them. They wouldn't be polite. They'd be enumerating which of his major organs they were going to pierce with bullets. So she was probably telling the truth.

*Don't pause. Act. Pausing gets you killed. Jump through the window. Worry about the landing in the air.* Again age--wisdom some might say--convinced him otherwise.

Ian didn't say a word, but came out from his hiding space. The woman was dressed in a suit: grey, severe, just enough slit in the skirt to let you know that she was a distraction. Her expression was pleasant but unreadable. She stood waiting, hands in front of her, clasped palm to palm.

Ian stepped up and gestured. She smiled, nodded, and led the way.

Where a blank, concrete wall had been, there was now an opening to an elevator. She stood and let him enter first, then positioned herself like a proper distraction should, bent over in front of him to press the lower of the two unmarked buttons.

Ian kept his eyes up, off her impossibly toned ass. *Stay sharp. Look for the angle.* This had to be an interview. It wouldn't be the first time that the original job had just been a test, a smokescreen for the real deal. *Fine. Agree to the terms. Do the work. Go along with whatever they ask until you can get your depth. Once you understand what's going on, take the control back.*

It was always about control. They had it for the moment. That moment wouldn't last.

He laughed thinking about that moment. He's anything but in control now. Maybe he never was. Maybe his whole life was just a series of illusions, a set of dominos that he thought he could stop when he wanted to. Espionage is the business of lies; why did he ever think he knew the truth?

*Stupid, old man.*

The fall will kill him if he actually hits the ground. Stupid… Stupid. What got him here? He hadn't leapt out the window. What came later?

The doors slid open, and Ian was surprised to find a hallway chiseled from stone stretching so far he thought the corridor might span the earth's width. Yellow, phosphorescent lights were staggered the length of it. Striations in the rock followed him in waves. The woman led him down its length, passing under light after light. She walked with a knowing stride, elegant and confident in her form-fitting skirt. It was hypnotic and graceful, like she belonged in the sea, swaying back and forth. The woman glanced over her shoulder, and a knowing grin touched her lips before she turned away.

Ian tore his gaze from the woman's toned rear. *Jesus, keep your focus,* he reminded himself. *I must be getting old. She knows what she's doing and I've been around the block enough to know better.* Ian felt for his cell phone, but only found the holster. The reminder that he was out of touch and alone shattered the façade. *I've gotta get through this.*

The hall sloped, and they passed deeper into the earth where water began cascading down the carved sides, seeping from various levels of striated rock beds. Small, grated drains on the floor edges dispersed the water to some place unknown. *Aren't we too deep to be in the water table?* He'd never been much for geology, but he'd brushed up when the contractors drilled the wells for his ranch house in Oregon.

The woman didn't slow, and Ian resumed his pace. The walls began to glisten beneath the thin waterfalls, the rock beneath reflecting the light in shades of blue and purple. The thin sheen of water had grown to envelop the entirety of both sides and now shimmered like nothing he'd seen before.

Ian coughed into a balled fist, then asked, "Hey, lady, you mentioned an employer. Are we gonna meet any time soon, or should I have packed some leftovers?"

She stopped walking and turned to meet his gaze. "Hungry, are you?" She licked her lips as though savoring a memory, then turned back down the hall. "It isn't far." Her heels splashed in the thin sheet of water now flowing across the hall.

Ian had no choice, as much as he hated it. There was no way out. He followed her farther until she stopped, bit her finger, and pressed its bloody end against a flattened panel the size of a fist. It blended into its surroundings under the glistening water. A doorway slid in and she passed under the sheet of liquid without hesitation. Ian passed through after her, drenching himself. When he emerged on the other side, he was surprised to find the woman standing next to an obese man in archaic, royal garb flowing with deep purples and greens. Unlike any monarchy he knew of, this man wore an ornate kilt and green cloak. Other than that, he was bare-chested and hairless, seated in a stone chair with more ornate carvings than anything Ian had seen before. A stern face and bulbous nose peered down at him with an inner fury. Ian ran a hand over his forehead and through his hair, clearing the water from his vision.

*Wait, what about her?* He looked from one to the other. Neither seemed to have been touched by the water. No other doors or panels appeared around the chiseled, stone room. The water flowed here, as it had in the hall, but neither of them seemed bothered by it. Looking between the two, he noticed something he hadn't seen before. They shared the same deep-purple eyes and a hungry glare.

*How could I have missed that?* A vision of her well-formed rear entered his thoughts. *Stupid, old man!*

Ian's heart skipped a beat, and he glanced nervously at the walls: no windows anywhere. He turned to retreat and found a muscle-bound man blocking his way. The black suit and sunglasses seemed out of place, but it was apparent what the man's function was. The door swung shut after his silent entrance, sealing Ian in like a rat in the sewer. The only differences were the flickering colors and the luminescent lights above. Even the nauseating smell returned in this room.

The absence of light seemed permanent, and the cold wind slapping his face was damp, not like the air he'd felt at altitude. *Where am I?*

"Where you are, is in my audience chamber." The voice was deep and powerful. His words lapped on the back of his teeth like tidal waves on the shore.

*I know I've never heard that voice before, and yet it feels familiar. Wait, did I ask that out loud before? I'm sure I didn't. How did...*

"How isn't important right now. Are you going to introduce yourself? I grow bored of this interview already."

*Regain your composure, old man.* "My name is Ian Masters. I apologize for my rudeness. This is all just so surreal. How would you prefer to be addressed, Sir?"

"You may refer to me as Your Highness," the large man replied. The woman leaned in and whispered into his ear, then he continued. "So, Mr. Masters is it?" His voice carried a deep, cold hatred at the utterance of the name. "Why give me such an obvious lie? You were caught in the basement uplinking Dawbry's mainframe with whoever your benefactors are. You accepted going deep into the bowels of the earth for an interview. And, more impressively, you reacted to my presence with only a brief moment of panic. You are no EPA investigator." He leaned closer and the combination of fish, brine, and brimstone wafted on his breath. "Who are you really?"

"Your Highness's observations are astute." *Got to think quickly, I need an old, verifiable ID.* "The name is Daniel Simmons. I'm a private investigator. The locals hired me to get info for the case they're bringing against Dawbry."

The woman smiled, almost seeming to purr. "John, who are you really working for? We will get the information from you, but I promise it will be much more fun if you cooperate."

*I think that's my name, but how does she know it?*

"I don't know who you think I am, but you're sadly mistaken. My name is Dan." The lie didn't even sound convincing to Ian… John; he still wasn't certain who he was. His voice cracked as panic started to sink in. "M-M-Maybe we could get some coffee when this is over, but I think I should be leaving." Before he could turn, two large, cold hands grabbed his shoulders from behind.

"Take him to my office… by Your Highness's leave, of course," added the attractive woman in a voice that had lost all sense of compassion.

"Do what you must, Arielle. I'll expect your report soon."

Unable to do more than protest, the goliath shoved Ian through the wall of water. By the time his eyes cleared, he was alone in a room with Arielle. Seaweed wraps entangled his arms, holding him firmly to a small stool

*How the hell did I get here?* It was as though the minutes faded into hours, leaving him with less than a memory.

The room was featureless, and for all Ian knew, he could be inside an egg. Stark, white walls seemed to flow in an oval. The only furniture, other than the stool, was a low table that Arielle sat perched atop, legs crossed as though the world could crumble around her, and she wouldn't bat an eyelash. Her smile was gone, vanished like so many unexplainable things. Everything that was once sultry had become predatory. She was a shark and Ian, a minnow. For the first time in many years, a trickle of nervous sweat rolled down Ian's temple.

*Get a grip. There's a way out. There always is.*

"Who do you work for," asked Arielle, wasting no time on simple chit-chat.

"You seem like you can read my mind," Ian retorted. "You tell me." *I don't believe the words I'm saying. It's an expression of speech,* he reminded himself. *But it's one that fits.*

"I would," she replied. "But you're a strong man, John. You have so many thoughts in your head and you can't keep them all in that basket of a brain. I'm only catching the ones that trickle over the brim. But the ones you've got floating down at the bottom… no, can't reach those."

Arielle slid from the table to stand in front of Ian, peering into his eyes. *How did I miss those sunken cheeks? The glint in her eyes that says she could gut me with one hand and talk on the phone to her mother with the other? The incisors that would make Dracula jealous? What have you gotten yourself into, old man?*

Arielle dragged her hand over the table as she took a step forward. The scrape echoed in the small room until her hand fell on a knife. Lifting it up, she admired her reflection for a moment. The blade itself was thin, nothing like the one in John's boot. His was meant to make horrid punctures that refuse to stop bleeding. Hers was made to peel back the most delicate of flesh with minimum trauma, a fillet knife.

*I really don't like where this is going. But I still have the knife in my boot. That hideaway sheath was the best investment I ever made.*

*It's not over yet, not till the pig's roasted, party goers are stuffed to the brim, and the fat lady can't sing another note.*

Arielle lazily regarded the edge of her shiny tool. "I wanted to reward you, John. I wanted you to tell me everything your mercenary heart had to say, and I wanted to give you warm, soft, and wet gratitude in return. Now, I have to play with things you were never meant to see outside your body. It isn't what I intended, but we all have our jobs to do, unless you tell me, right now, who… do… you… work… for?"

Ian struggled to come up with something, anything, and finally resorted to the truth, hoping it would buy some time. "I don't know. I worked through intermediaries. They just called it the 'agency'. The money was good, so I didn't ask for more."

Arielle stopped just past the table. *Closer, but not close enough, yet.* Cocking her head to the side, she gave him an unreadable look. In those fleeting moments, Ian guessed what she was thinking; something to do with which part of him would look best minus some skin.

"I believe you," she said after a moment's pause. "But you're going to have to tell me more."

*Time to switch tactics.* "I don't have to tell you jack," he spat. "I'm going to end up bait in the river, and you know it. There's not a damn reason I should make this easier for you."

With a twist of his ankle, Ian tested the straps as though struggling to break free. The wraps tying his legs to the chair were tight, but slick. Aware of what needed to be done, his last chance at survival, he waited for the proper moment.

She stepped toward him in slow, graceful strides. The knife flashed and Ian was instantly bleeding from both cheeks before he could blink.

Stepping back to the table, Arielle picked up a small vial. She popped the stopper off with a thumb, then flung it into his face. The cuts lit up like neon, and pain coursed through his veins.

Over his hissing screams, she yelled, "Reason enough for you?"

Ian gritted his teeth and managed, "Nope. Need a better one."

Laughter erupted from the woman like a bubbling furnace: another uncomfortable sound. *That's not good. I want her mad, not amused.*

"Oh, this is going to be a long, entertaining night isn't it," she said through her mirth.

"Does that mean I get a lap dance?" asked Ian. Writhing in his chair, he loosened the binding around his good leg.

"No, but you do get this."

Arielle flew at him like lightning and her fist slammed into Ian's gut like a well-manicured Volkswagen.

Blood flew from his mouth, spattering the white room, and was closely followed by, "Please, miss, may I have another?"

The purple-eyed woman granted his wish. Ian rolled with it and stifled a smile as his leg almost slipped free of the slimy bonds.

"Wanna go for the bonus round, sweetheart?" asked Ian. His voice was patronizing, but the anguish stretched across his face told another story. He couldn't take another shot, and he knew it.

Arielle screamed and lunged at him. *This one's going to shatter my pancreas,* Ian thought with certainty, *but I have other plans.* His leg pulled up and out of the bindings. Pushing away from her, he rolled to the floor, compressed like a spring waiting for the right moment. Realizing her punch landed on nothing but air, she turned her momentum and fell on Ian like a tiger pursuing its dinner. Ian slid his free calf against the still-bound foot, catching the heel of his shoe and the pommel of his boot knife. With an instantaneous jerk, the blade ejected itself through the bottom of the sheath and four inches past his boot sole.

A widening of her eyes revealed her astonishment as Ian thrust his bladed foot into her chest. Seconds seemed like painful minutes as Arielle's quivering form weighed on Ian's foot. But eventually, her wide-eyed stare darkened, and her quivering form went limp.

*I don't have much time. They've got to be watching.* Pushing her back with his free leg, the blade tugged at what was left of the sheath but stayed dangling from his ankle. The years hadn't yet stolen his flexibility, so Ian pulled his ankle up to his left hand and began slicing at the remaining bonds. The first restraint was awkward to cut, but the others rapidly disappeared with just a single stroke *At least two minutes have passed. The guards will be here any moment.*

The walls appeared smooth. The spot behind Ian should have had a door, but he couldn't discern one. Peering around him, he scanned the table in the hopes of finding a button or control; something that would give him a viable egress from this prison.

The only things he found were more implements of torture, a host of tools: pointy, hooked, and sharp. There were three syringes, each one filled with an ochre fluid. Thinking quickly, Ian grabbed one and slid it into his pocket.

*It might be evidence of what they produce here. I know it's a long shot, but it's a spot above where I stand now, which is empty handed.*

Minute four passed, and Ian began to panic. That's when he heard the scraping.

Turning in place, a nightmare appeared before him with horrible, feral claws and teeth. Arielle was moving when she should have been nothing more than grub fertilizer.

Ian backed into the wall. *I can't believe it. This can't be real.*

She screamed and lurched for the table, her face now more beast than beauty. She grabbed one of the other two syringes and jabbed it into her own neck. Ian's stomach turned a somersault as the bleeding wound in her chest began to bubble with yellow froth and seal itself.

His composure broke. Turning in place, Ian slammed his shoulder into the wall. It gave, but only a little. In panic, he slammed into it again and the wall gave way like tearing through chicken skin. Through the wall, Ian fell to the floor of another unknown room with walls like the previous.

*Oh, man. I'm not just one room away from where I met His Twisted Majesty. How long was I out? It could take ages to escape this place.*

Peering around him, Ian spotted stairs going up. Glancing over his shoulder, he spotted Arielle getting to her feet and looking at him through the tattered wall with a much more substantial knife in her hand than the boot knife in his.

He scrambled to his feet and ran without a thought more. His lungs burned as he topped the fourth flight of stairs at full sprint.

A Klaxon sound echoed above, saying "The prisoner has escaped."

With no time to rest, Ian tried the two doors that appeared before him, but behind each one a horde of boots and shouts warned him away. From two floors below, Arielle bellowed, "He's here!"

*Up's the only way left.*

Rounding the stairs, he chanced on a door that looked normal enough, with no sounds behind it. Ian pushed through to find normal-looking office doors lining both sides of the hall. Ian tried the first, but it barely jiggled. Pulling a wire and card from his pocket, he paused to try to pick one, but paused too long.

The hiss of an opening door alerted him to the vicious bitch's approach, her blade out in front, leading the way to him. He deflected it by reflex, but not fast enough. Rather than sliding to the side and innocently avoiding his tender bits, it impaled his spleen.

Ian counterstruck automatically. Her neck gave way to the edge of his knife with a sickening gurgle, and her eyes died a second time that night.

*But what if she comes back?* Ian wondered. Unwilling to take the chance, his knife struck out a dozen more times as he yelled, "Stay dead."

As his thrumming heart slowed, the pain in his side returned. He felt where her knife had momentarily embedded itself in his side, and his hand came away coated with warm blood… his blood. Boots echoed up the stairs, mere feet away, and from somewhere else on the floor came the ping of an elevator opening.

*This isn't how I want to spend my last moments.* Ian's mind flashed back to the syringe. *Don't think, old man, just do.* The needle stung like pissed-off fire as it sunk into Ian's neck. He pushed the plunger and instantly his skin tried to crawl off his bones. Nausea engulfed him, but overshadowing that was a feeling of pure strength.

Boot heels smacking on tile forced Ian up. No time to question it further, Ian leaped at the first door and bashed it open. An empty office greeted him with a large open window and a window washer's scaffolding outside. *It's a jump, but I can make it. I'm sure of it.*

Bullets smacked the doorframe and all questions fled. He had no choice. He ran headlong for the window and everything slowed down. His senses became heightened with the adrenaline rush. Bullets whizzed past him, and Ian counted thirteen motes of dust. His senses were so aware he could feel every hair on his body, every thread of the clothes touching his skin.

As his feet left the windowsill for the second jump, his thoughts turned back to his flight. He landed on the platform with a hard thump, and as the scaffolding swayed, he held the knife away from his body. The last thing he needed was to become a human pincushion, his life ended suddenly on his own knife.

Bullets pinged off the frame as he hit the controls. In the sunlight the sky was so bright, he could barely see. *There's a lever on this contraption. It'll make the thing descend faster; if I can just find it...* His hands flew over the controls in a millisecond. It wasn't hard to find. Time was so stretched that every second seemed like an intermission.

As another barrage of bullets thundered around Ian, he felt the lever under his hand. *No time like the present,* he thought with a laugh and pulled. The bullets flew around Ian like a hailstorm. Even in his enhanced state, all sense of direction eluded him, and the brightness turned to black.

Bullets slammed into his flesh, one… two… three. The wind whipped at him from below, reminding him that he was falling. *Is that good or bad?* he wondered, unable to connect the dots that led him to that moment. Bullets clanged on the cable holding the platform up. A distinct twang sent a shudder through the scaffolding and the platform upended.


*Oh, that's when the falling started. Good to know.*

A voice echoes through the void. "It's falling, plummeting."

"I know I'm falling dammit…! Wait, who the hell's that?" asks John, but the urgent voice continues without hearing him.

"The N.S. isn't enough. Push fluids!"

Light speckles John's vision.

"Get his damned clothes off, and get me four units of O-negative, stat. He's bleeding out."

Something jerks at John's suit pants, and as they're cut away, air greets his exposed body. The wind rushing past has calmed, merging with the hum and beep of machines clustered around him. His vision slowly returns and the spots disappear. Gravity still pulls at him, though, rushing toward his head in his awkward position. His sneakers perch above him on the tilted table and beyond that, a stark, white ceiling.

"Who is he?" asks an older nurse with gray-tinged hair from across the room.

"God knows, but he's lucky to be alive. Where is that O.R. team? Get Doctor Ralin on the phone."

"On it," squeaks a slim man with a five-o'clock shadow and green scrubs. The others ignore him as he mutters into the phone.

Applying pressure to a compress on his side, the nurse mumbles, "That fall should've killed him. I think landing on the scaffold might have saved his life."

A fragile blonde outfitted in more green scrubs interrupts. "Should his innards be foaming like that?"

John tries to fight gravity and leans forward. A groan escapes his lips. "A-a-am I still falling?" The effort triggers a bloody cough.

"Enough, Irene. We'll have it tested," answers the deep voice that broke through the darkness. The man grips John's rising shoulders and forces him back down. A square of white covers his mouth and nose. As their eyes meet, a shiver runs through the patient. The doctor's purple eyes peer down, weighing John like a scale, but to what end?

*Oh, no. Not again.*

"Don't try to say too much. You're not falling. The ground took care of that. Do you know your name?" asks the man in a soothing voice.

Ian... John... Dan... Paul... Sam... and a dozen more names filter through John's hazy brain. *Which is mine?*

"N-n-no," he mutters in a staggered breath.

## Unseen

"Have you ever noticed how many references there are to an unseen world? TV, movies, books, they seem obsessed with it. One moment we're going through the looking glass or through Spare Room via Ward Robe, and the next we're not in Kansas anymore, running from Fae or worse. Why is that? Is it literary convention, or is there more to it? Is it something buried in our collective unconscious trying to be heard again?"

"These sort of conversations are exactly why I'm never giving you coffee at midnight again." Sasha throws a sugar packet at me, clearly annoyed but so radiant in the full moonlight that I can't be bothered to care. "We always end up somewhere we probably shouldn't be with you spouting off nonsense, all because you can't sleep. Some of us have to work tomorrow."

The blue light softens her features, but the shadows give her a terrifying visage. I'm taken aback. "My Dark Queen, I have offended." I bow deeply and back away. "How can your humble Jester make amends?"

*Giggle.* I love that sound. She pulls herself up, getting into character. "Jerrel, you are an unworthy cur. I have half a mind to banish you from my court. Why should I retain your services?"

A sly grin steals across my face, "Because, My Queen, your other half of mind would miss me terribly." I laugh and duck another sugar packet, tumbling through the night. I fall over something, and she laughs heartily. I go over to inspect the obstacle and find a small statue. It stands no more than a foot high and appears to be carved of wood.

It moves slowly, and a dusty voice comes from the statue, "My Queen, if your fool is done attempting to crush me, might I have a moment? I must admit I did not recognize so brilliant a disguise. Had I know you had come to the mortal realm, I would have had myself properly announced."

At first, I wonder if it is but a bit of dream that I forgot to put away when I made the bed this morning. Then I consider that this might be some elaborate prank, a set-up for some website where a host steps out and announces that I've been punked. But as the statue begins to move in my hands, the legs and arms creaking and expanding, I begin to accept that this is really happening.

The little figure pushes out of my palm and rolls backwards off my fingertips. He tumbles in the air, and then lands on the balls of his feet in the grass. Stretching himself, he stands, but comes just past my waist now.

I turn back to Sasha. Smiling, she says, "How are you doing that? I know you didn't slip anything into my mocha because you would have told me, but this is the best trick I've ever seen you pull."

I shake my head. "This isn't me."

I turn back and find myself staring eye-to-eye with a face that looks half carved and half grown. He says in a rich and baritone voice, "Of course it's not your doing. I was here long before you, and I will still be here when you are but a memory so distant, Our Queen will wonder if she knew you or dreamt you."

I stand, puzzled. "Jerrel, this is impressive," says Sasha, "but it's rapidly losing its amusement. Stop it. I want to go home."

I step back. The statue, now golem, has no malice in its face, but does seem menacing. It's as though the creature's just doing a job and nothing more. Sasha's dismay is palpable and makes me want to tell her to run, but I hesitate. This strange, earthen manifestation might be prepared to give chase.

His expression is puzzled as he looks from her, to me, and back. He rumbles, "My Queen, this fool does not know the way to your realm. Here, let me help you. I will carry you there on my back if you wish it."

He steps forward and Sasha kicks out her feet, backing up on the hood of my Pathfinder. Her coffee spills, falling to the ground... cup and all. Fear glimmers in her eyes as the reality of this thing that would be her servant and transport finally sets in.

I look to my right. The trees have changed as well. Two young ashes have bent their trunks, coming together to form an archway. The space between them grows dark as pitch, though I can see into the woods well to the side of either. The sound of sinister calliope and faint whiffs of sweet, heavy incense carry to me on the wind.

Turning back, Sasha is nearly mad with panic. I *have* to do something.

Two steps and I am between my love and this strange, creaking man. Reaching into my pocket, I draw forth my folding knife. I never thought I'd draw it on anything more troubling than a case of canned peaches. It opens with a flick of my thumb, and I hold my arms out in an open stance of challenge.

"Not one more step," I demand. "Take another and I shall shave you to kindling."

The wooden statue, now a wooden man a head taller than me, says, "Of course. I should not have thought to touch my Queen without first proving myself worthy. Very well then, fool. You will be the instrument I use to demonstrate my worthiness to She Who Sits In Twilight."

His words weigh down my knife as though empowering gravity to pull my hand to the ground. What did he say? She Who Sits In Twilight... Sasha? Before I can muster an answer, the imposing figure lunges forward, jolting me into the front of the SUV. I bat his tendril-like hand away with the knife. It scrapes the veins of wood. Embedding itself in a rough crack, the silver blade snaps under the pressure. It does little more than redirect the golem's thrust, but it's enough. Summoning my varsity football training, I scramble around its stumpy legs and slam my shoulder beneath its arm like a linebacker. Coach Morgan would be proud. The root-like legs lift, but rather than plough the thing into the ground, the unnatural archway beckons me forward with a twinkle deep within its shadowy void.

"Boy, what are you thinking?" rasps the monster, his voice like the wind rustling through scraping tree limbs.

I hold firm, arms wrapped around the creature's trunk. Rather than wriggle beneath my grasp, the creature's arms and face begin flowing along the trunk like leaves sticking out of a pond. The bark under my fingers gurgles and, before I can reach the arch, his face shifts to within mere inches of mine.

"I see you know the way," whispers the golem. "But I cannot leave the Queen."

Suddenly, my forward momentum stops. My feet plough troughs in the ground, my sneakers digging into the moist soil. It's like the being is rooted in the ground. A disheartening glance below confirms my suspicions. One of the creature's feet has grown much longer than the other in a matter of seconds. Its skinny roots throb in the moonlit night, pulsating and growing as they suck nutrients from the soil. I try to pull away, but his arms and free leg encompass me.

"Oh no, do not flee youngling. I am not done with you. I'm hungry." His sinuous limbs grasp tighter, flowing around me like layers of rope. What would have taken decades for a real tree to accomplish, this creature does in seconds. His torso grows, enveloping me.

Half my face is encompassed by the wooden figure, and I can't move. "Sasha, help!" I shout through a partially bark-covered mouth. I scan the area with my one free eye and spot the vehicle at the corner of my sight. Sasha's screams turn to moans and she begins thrashing. What's happening? I can't move to help. Then, the seizure stops. After a brief moment of stillness, she takes in a deep breath. A blood-curdling screams erupts from her thin body. Through my panic, the sound drifts to my unclogged ear, turning into a haggard, teetering laugh that echoes through the wind like morbid wind chimes. It's Sasha's voice, but with a playful malevolence I've never heard.

"Oh, Timber, will you wait a moment?" she asks as though ordering a Danish from a waiter. At her request, Timber's pulsing growth stops, but doesn't recede. Unable to move, I watch Sasha's limber figure dance into view. She laughs hysterically when she gets within arm's reach. If I could move, I could stroke her porcelain cheek. But the look she turns on me isn't Sasha's. Her crazed eyes belong to someone else.

"Wow, Jerrel, you really have a nice profile. Although, you do appear a bit terrified." Striking a solemn, melodramatic pose, she covers half her face with a hand. Then, her visible profile breaks into a wide grin and the crazy twinkle returns to her dark eye.

47

Is this the woman I love? "Sasha, what's goin' on?" The part of my face engorged in bark refuses to cooperate, as though numb with anesthetic. The muddled words are lilting, but audible.

"On?" she asks in mock confusion. "Why, we were having a great evening. That is, until you began ridiculing my very existence." An irritated and shaky hand ejects a Virginia Slim from the pack. "Do you mind?" she asks. Timber extends two tendrils, flicks them together, and a small flame leaps into being at the edge of his splintered finger.

"What?" I ask, attempting to ignore the odd gesture as Sasha puffs at the cigarette.

"You see," she continues between breaths, "this has been a great holiday. I've loved spending time with you and hoped you might even come back with me. But now I see that you could care less about fairy tales, myths, and fantasy. With all of our teasing and role-playing, I would've thought you figured it out. I wasn't joking when I introduced myself as Queen of the Night that day in the restaurant." A fleeting look of pity flashes across her face and then vanishes. "Now, my vacation is ruined, and you... such a disappointment."

To Timber, she continues, "Finish up. You'll need your energy for the trip. Then, you will get your audience." On her orders, the gurgling begins again. A forced smile creeps up Sasha's lips as my view of her is slowly enveloped.

"But I love you," I try to answer.

"So I thought," she mumbles. "Sasha loves you too, but little did she realize who was sharing her body. I've enjoyed it while it's lasted. It's quite a nice shape; robust in the chest." The queen slaps her breasts for emphasis; then winces. "It will be a shame to leave her so broken and fragile." With a shrug, she flutters her hand at Timber and drifts from view. As my sight dims, her intakes of breath and the crackle of burning tobacco mingle with the crickets until even sound is drowned out.

## Night Eyes

Everyone has something about themselves that they're proud of. They have some skill, talent, or natural ability that sets them apart. For me, I have fantastic night vision. I'm not saying that I can see in pitch darkness or that I have one over on the family cat, but I can pick out details in far less light than most people. It's a hard power to flaunt. I do get to use it occasionally. On a full moon without much cloud cover, I'll take my car down seldom-used country roads with the headlights off. I know it sounds dangerous, but any other vehicles would have their lights on, so I can avoid them. Large animals aren't as likely to freeze in the road if they aren't spotlighted. Plus, my vision is that damn good.

I got to indulge in this pleasure last week. It was about 1:30 in the morning, and I was coming home from an evening of winning at cards. I had the windows down to clear the smoke from my lungs and let the cool, crisp, spring air keep me sharp on my moonlit journey. I pulled smoothly through a blind S-curve in the road only to catch a flickering, orange light over the embankment. If my lights had been on, there's no chance I would have noticed. I parked my car on a gravel road that led down the side of the bank, got out, and made my way down the embankment toward the fire. A horror scene lay before me. An unmarked, armored car lay on its side, ripped open, and blazing in the moonlight. I ran to the wrecked vehicle and found two guards dead and one dying. "It's going to be alright. I'm calling for help," I assured him after rushing to his side.

"Son, there's no signal here. That's why they chose it." The man was interrupted by an episode of bloody coughing. "What's your name, Son?"

"Jackson."

"Well Jackson, can I trust you to fill a dying man's last wish?"

I stammered, "You're not dying. I'm going to get you some help."

He held up one hand and beckoned me closer. "It won't get here in time. They won't let it. But, they didn't know what they were looking for. They took the lock-boxes, but it was on me the whole time." He pressed something into my hand. "Go. Take this and call the number on the card. Mr. Daniels will make it worth your while." Another cough and he continued, obviously weakened from speaking. "Take some of the cash too. No sense in letting it burn. Hurry, I don't know how long it'll be before they realize their mistake."

"I can do that. What's your name?"

"Walter Jackson." It came as a whisper. The fierce light that was in his eyes seconds before was replaced by a dull reflection of the flames. I ran into the wreckage and grabbed a full brick of cash that had yet to ignite and made it back to my car, smokier than ever. The whole situation was so confusing. Tears streamed down my face for a stranger, yet I was richer than I'd ever dreamed.

I drove home with the lights on and slid into a hot shower. I must have dozed beneath the steaming water, because the cold of an empty water heater brought me to my senses. I went to the kitchen and poured a cup of tea. As it steeped, I examined what I'd been given. It was a non-descript flash drive and a business card. The card was solid black save for bronze lettering that said 'Mr. Daniels (201)555-7933.'

The bound stack of hundreds lay next to it, the edges tinged with black from the close proximity to the fire. I ignored the bundle and stared at the nondescript card.

Who had Walter meant... "*they* didn't know what they were looking for"? I didn't know, but had to do as Mr. Jackson asked. It was his dying wish.

Pulling my cell from my pants pocket, I dialed the number. It rang twice, then a groggy voice demanded, "Trouble?"

"Y-yeah, something like that," I stuttered. "Are you Mr. Daniels?"

"Of course I am," he spat back. "Who the hell else would pick up this phone?"

I wasn't sure. Was it a cell or landline? Who knew? "Walter said *they* mistakenly took the lock boxes instead of what they were after."

"Shit! Well, where's Walter?"

"Dead," I replied. The word echoed through the kitchen as though I'd had something to do with it.

"I see," answered the man, considering the predicament. "And who are you?"

What was I supposed to say? I didn't know this guy from my mail man. Giving my name to a dying armored truck guard was one thing. This was entirely another. "Uhhh... I'd rather not say until I know what's going on."

"Well that's not going to happen, kid. I can find out who you are, where you live, and the name of your parents' Cocker Spaniel in less than two minutes. So, give it up. What happened and how did you get my number?"

My mother was deathly afraid of dogs and wouldn't have one within a hundred yards of the house, but I got his meaning. "Look, Mister. I came across Mr. Jackson's armored truck on Route 33 last night. He was the only guard still moving, but that didn't last long. He gave me a flash drive and your card. Said to fulfill his dying wish by calling you up. That you'd make it worth my while."

I didn't mention the money sitting on the counter. The most I'd ever seen working at the Chicken Shack had been a couple thousand in ones, fives, and twenties after the local high school won the state championship. Cars had flooded the fast-food joint flaunting deer antlers on their car hoods and shouting, "Go Cumberland!" and "The Bucks rule!" The small pile of hundreds on the table was more money than I'd ever seen in one place. Maybe more would be forthcoming.

"Okay, Mr. Jackson. You related to Walter?" asked the man.

"What... no... how'd you know my name?"

"I lied. It would take the cops two minutes, and we're far better than them."

A frog suddenly leapt into my throat. Who was I dealing with? "Look, Mr. Daniels," I croaked. "I don't know what this is all about. I'd just like to do as Walter asked and maybe get something for my time."

"All right. How's two grand and you don't say a word to anybody?" answered Mr. Daniels with a hearty chuckle.

"That's fine," I replied, sipping my tea and working the lump from my throat. "Where do you want to meet?"

"No time for that. I've got a man on his way. He'll be at your door in five."

"Minutes?" I squeaked and grabbed a T-shirt off the back of the kitchen chair.

"No, hours… of course minutes. God, you really are clueless."

Then, three loud knuckle-splitting thumps rattled my door. "Jeez, that was more like five seconds."

"Wait!" shouted Mr. Daniels. "What was that?"

I threw the bundle of money into my room, shut the door, and scooped the flash drive up before heading to the door. "Someone's at the door. Your man must already be here."

"No, wait…" he replied, but before I reached the door, something crashed against it.

The wooden frame creaked, but held. Then, the second crash spun the door into the wall. I halted in the middle of the living room. A large Asian man, too broad for the doorway, shouldered his way through. He wore a dark suit that must have been tailored at Bodybuilders-R-Us and black Ray-Bans that barely squeezed onto his bulbous head. Suddenly, I knew who *they* were, and I wasn't sticking around to end up like Walter. Pocketing the drive, I leapt out the window and onto the fire escape shouting into the phone, "*They're* here. Did you hear me, Daniels? *They're* freaking here!"

I didn't wait to see how the muscle-bound monster got through the small apartment window. Instead, I rocketed up the metal staircase and into the night. At least out here we'd be on my turf, and I'd have the advantage.

"Okay, how many of them are there?" demanded Daniels.

"One goon the size of a freakin' freight train," I stammered, taking the last steps onto the roof.

This was a place I knew well. Ol' Man Leary was always feeding his pigeons up here. He was blind as a bat, but loved to hear my stories. To my surprise, Mr. Leary stood in the large bird cage that very night, dressed in a checkered red and black robe and shuffling bird seed through his fingers.

"Hey there, Jackson," creaked Ol' Man Leary between bird coos. "Thought you might be up tonight."

"But how...?"

I halted at the odd sight. If that brute made it up to Mr. Leary, he'd never stand a chance. Mr. Leary turned from the cage with one hand cupped over the other. The seeds stopped raining from his fingers, and now a faint blue glow seeped through them.

"Come here, boy," croaked the man. "You can see this, can't you?"

I nodded.

"That's a good boy. Come take it before that cretin makes it up the steps."

I couldn't see what was within his hands, but the glow somehow beckoned me forth. I followed its soundless call as though in a trance.

"Jackson, where are you? Jackson!" Mr. Daniels screamed through the phone, but I flipped it shut and slid it into my pocket. Something else in my pocket was growing warm. I pulled it out. The flash drive hummed pleasantly the closer I got.

A heavy grunt sounded behind me as the metal stairs rattled. Ol' Man Leary's attention turned toward the approaching brute and, with a nod, something skittered out of the cage, flying behind me. I didn't care. The only thing that mattered was what the old man held in his hands. When I was within a foot, the flash drive began steaming, but my gut said this was supposed to happen. I wasn't sure how I knew, but it felt right.

In fact, everything felt like it was in its proper place. Underneath my panic, there was a pervasive calm rooting me to the earth, making every step I took seem exactly like the last one. It was like the first time I took Ecstasy….

Oh, crap. I'd been drugged; something on the outside of the flash drive.

I looked at Mr. Leary's face. Beneath his milky eyes was a wide grin that suggested he was tripping right along with me, even though that made not the slightest bit of sense.

He opened his hands and a vial of luminous liquid sat cradled in his palm. Behind me were the squawks of birds and vulgar, shouted words, but they were muffled as though a thick blanket were hanging between us. My pursuer and the steaming flash drive were nearly forgotten as I studied the vial, entranced by the phosphorescence.

"You've got the catalyst," Mr. Leary said. "But this is the real deal. And you're going to need both soon. But you should move. Now!"

I started to ask why, but he tossed the vial at me. I had to step to my right to catch it and almost dropped the flash drive. While juggling the two objects, the Asian brick's fist flashed where my head had been. Somehow he'd gotten away from the attack pigeons. His sunglasses had disappeared, and it looked like the birds played tic-tac-toe on his cheeks. But that wasn't the weird part; his eyes were the same milky white as Leary's.

I saw another punch coming before he so much as twitched his shoulder. I stepped back and to my right again to avoid it and check on Leary, but he was gone. The door he'd gone through stood open, but tall, dark, and murderous was in my way.

I turned and ran for the edge of the building. I'd figure out where I was going when I got there. Maybe I'd even discover how the blind guy was following me later, too.

The muscle-bound cretin's steps shook the roof as he gave chase. The faint, tinny voice of Mr. Daniels echoed from my pocket. Evidently the phone hadn't hung up, but with the brute on my tail and a ledge appearing before me, all thoughts of Mr. Daniels fled. I could almost hear the Asian's breath coming up from behind, so I jumped.

I don't know why the hell trying to span the alleyway seemed like a good idea, but it did. I landed one floor down on the opposite fire escape. I glanced over my shoulder for half a second and saw the Asian sailing through the air straight toward me.

Without thought, I threw my forearms over my face and dove through someone's apartment window just before the meatstick landed. Two kids looked up from the TV and gawked at me.

"Is this building's basement unlocked?" I asked, pulling a few pieces of glass from my arms.

The elder shook his head. Then the younger one screamed. As the Asian stuffed himself through the window, I made for the door.

I found the fire stairs quickly and leaped down them three at a time. I pulled ahead, but only a little.

"I'm gonna jerk your scrawny head off, you little insect," the Asian bellowed.

"Got to catch me first," I shouted.

## Strange Circumstances

The flash drive was smoking like a teenager in the school bathroom and the vial was clenched in my fist so hard that I was afraid the thick, cool glass would crack. But I felt amazing. Something jazzed me up on that roof, though I still had no idea where this was going. The anxiety of where it may lead was something no shift at the Chicken Coupe could ever compare to.

My first thought had been to get where I could put my eyes to my advantage. The fact that the guy trying to murder me was blind made me less confident in that plan. But downstairs, I could find the Laundromat or the boiler room or someplace with enough white noise that he couldn't track me by sound.

It wasn't much of a plan, but it was what I had.

As I flew down the last flight of stairs, I threw my body against the basement door. It opened and I stumbled down the short flight of steps into the room. Chancing a look back, the Asian peered my way and started prowling up the hall. In a panic, I leaped to my feet and found the light switch, flicking it off.

There was an HVAC unit down there. A collection of pipes creaked and the sound of water trickling through added to the ambience. There was even the hum of a fuse box. I got behind a support beam and squatted down to think. What next? Where could I go?

I looked at the items that had turned my poker night into a run for my life. The blue vial was just what it had been on the roof. The flash drive had changed, like a melted Hershey's miniature in my hand. As the plastic sloughed off, something other than a little solid-state bit of electronics revealed itself. Whoever hid this did a damned good job.

It was a straw made of something that looked gold but felt like steel. The catalyst, Mr. Leary had said.

I looked at the vial. The tube would fit in the neck perfectly.

What I did next, I did on autopilot. Small crystals lined the inside of the straw, the source of the fumes. I popped the top off the vial and, sure enough, the straw fit into place. I put it up one nostril, then the other, inhaling deeply on each.

No calm I'd ever felt compared to this. I was the Earth and all the stars were well-set in heaven. Nothing was a surprise, but everything was a discovery. I was the column I was leaning on, the clothes on my body, the floor beneath my feet, and the murderer about to come through the door.

Wait, murderer? Time to duck.

The concrete shook from the force of his punch. He stomped as I rolled out of the way. I took a step back and his fist took up the space where my head had just been. I dodged left and his next punch landed on air.

I could feel the strikes before they were launched. I knew where to step before the signal was sent to me feet. I was at one with everything and the world was my playground.

I swung my foot up and sent a size-10, steel-toed boot into the Asian's fortune cookies. It should have crumpled him, but he caught my ankle in his thighs and fell back; I had to follow.

I knew if he twisted, my legs were broken and every other bone I had to follow. I shot my other foot at his knee and he grunted as the cartilage shattered.

I rolled back and stood up.

"You worm," he said. "You inhaled the vapors! You unworthy waste of flesh, how dare you?"

"I dare a lot. Like this."

I ran again. He scrambled up behind me, but not before I made it into the hall. When I got to the doorway, someone killed the lights in the hall, but down by the elevators four guys were coming with pistols drawn.

A shuffling step alerted me to the Asian approaching from behind. I flipped the light switch and dropped to the floor.

The guys ahead spotted the Asian and unloaded their guns at him; the bullets thumped into his chest with the sound of suction cups.

I looked up to find them bearing down on me, guns leveled, but no one drilled me with bullets. I couldn't see their faces, but understood who they were in an instant even with my night vision somehow failing; Mr. Daniels's men, come for his magic tube. The look on their faces suggested I probably wouldn't get that extra two grand. In my mind's eye, I saw where they wanted to shoot me. But I also knew there was no reason to panic, although I couldn't explain why.

The reason for my feeling of security turned out to be Mr. Leary. He stepped from the fire stairs, his shabby rooftop couture exchanged in favor of a blue button-up and a pair of carpenter jeans. He was a wonder to behold, his doddering nature replaced with deadly confidence.

He wove through the four men like a snake through tree branches. An old kitchen knife protruded from one hand, and its blade found the throats of the men with the guns. It was as though he'd waltzed through them.

After he finished, he stepped up to me with a disturbing demeanor, but I knew it was intended for someone else. He felt like a friend, and I needed one right now. He offered a hand.

I took it. The lights seemed to have come back a bit.

Mr. Leary pulled my slightly-singed cash out of his pocket and said, "You should take this and get gone. Those jokers won't be the last."

I shook my head. "What the hell is going on?"

"Use a little of that stuff," he said, pointing at the vial in my hand with the straw still sticking out of it, "and you'll be able to see a few seconds into the future. Use a lot and you can see much more, but the cost is higher."

"Cost?" I asked.

He pulled one set of eyelids wide so I could see the milky white of his eyeball all the way around. "Warning," he said, "may be habit forming."

He gave a hearty laugh, and I shoved it into his hands. "The phone too," he muttered with an outstretched hand. "Trust me."

Mr. Leary had saved my life and given me a chance at a future. I didn't question it and handed the cell over. By the time I got to my car, I felt my usual self and the drug was no longer blinding me. I left town and didn't look back.

My night eyes were good enough for me.

## Free Doster

"It's a coffee shop, Dan." Vic's tone suggested that he was underwhelmed by the venue. "I haven't seen you in three years, and when I finally make it to the city, you bring me to a coffee shop?"

Dan leaned into his macchiato and said, "It's the airport's fault. You got in too late for lunch, too early for dinner, and hungry from a three-hour flight with no meal. I thought coffee and a scone might take the edge off until we make for Lugia's later. Plus, the Free Doster Rally is parading by here in about a half hour."

"Free Doster?"

"Do you live under a rock? Manchester is small, but you can get cable and the internet out there."

"I don't like the news. I watch cartoons, and the internet is for porn."

"So is Doster... He's some reclusive billionaire that no one's heard of until a few weeks ago. He was arrested, without a hearing, for conspiracy to rape an alien species."

Vic coughed. "Ha Ha! You almost had me there. There's no such law."

"That's precisely what the Free Doster people are saying. A rival human rights group is holding an anti-rally today. They call themselves SIR, the Society for Inhuman Rights." Dan flipped open his laptop. After a few quick key-strokes, he turned the screen to his friend.

US billionaire Kaplan Kirkwood Doster was imprisoned on 4/1/17. He was trying to gain the permission from NASA to launch his own deep-space mission with a small group of scientists and adventurers. The purpose of this venture was listed as, and I quote, 'We are going to have sex with the Orion Slave Girls.' What NASA took as a harmless April Fool's Day prank, the Department of Homeland Security took much more seriously. They stormed his Montana launch site and arrested Doster and his followers. The location of the prison is unknown, but Doster's security footage was leaked after the raid.

Vic took the laptop, absorbed in footage of secret, government raids and lawyers from both sides fighting on talk shows and news programs. The internet was abuzz with almost nothing else. He tapped at the keyboard while muttering, "Maybe I do live under a rock. Hey, did you see that a third group has put in a permit to assemble for this protest?"

"Who?" Dan retrieved his laptop from Vic.

"It's some local fetish group. They're protesting under the banner of 'Slave girls need love too.' I bet they're doing it just to wig out SIR." Vic sipped his now-cold coffee. "So, how's the government handling this?"

"The official position is that there's no one by that name in the US prison system, nor has anyone been able to find his birth record or Social Security Number. It seems like the entire record of his existence is online. But, an off-shore bank account hired some pretty high-powered lawyers in his name. This just infuriates the conspiracy theorists all the more. They claim that he was either using an alias when sending the request to NASA or that the government erased him. Depends on which end of the wacko pool you want to swim in."

Vic drained his cup and stood. "I'm getting a refill before they come by. Want one?" Dan nodded, once again buried in the 'net.

The coffee-shop waitress took their cups, and as she began refilling them, a bundled figure in the corner slid to the side of a booth to peer out the window. Her corduroy jacket was covered in dried leaves and travel stains. At her feet, a sign clattered to the floor. 'Slave girls for Cookies!' was plastered across the bright-pink poster board. The woman retrieved it from the floor and sat the sign on the seat beside her; then turned back to the window and the growing street crowd outside.

Vic took the steaming cups and maneuvered past the bedraggled woman out of curiosity. She didn't seem to notice when he accelerated past her and back to Dan. "Man, how many locos do you have out here?"

"What do you mean?" Dan asked, pulling his eyes from the screen.

"That woman in the corner has a protest sign and looks like she's waited her whole life for today. From the smell, I think she swore off bathing until Doster was either freed or killed too." Vic shook his head. "I'm really not sure which."

"Eh, this kind of thing brings the loonies out of the woodwork. She's probably just an extremist."

"Yeah... I'm sure, but for what side?"

Dan's attention had returned to the computer, but the second question gave him pause. Men and women began gathering outside the coffee shop's windows, signs with slogans of Doster for President perched over their shoulders. Across the street, a group of brutish women were gathering. One woman that might just have stepped off a construction site ripped open her flannel shirt to reveal a T-shirt advertising 'We are all Orion Slave Girls.' A few of her comrades slapped her on the back and began chanting, but the voices barely drifted through the coffee shop's busy doors.

Seeing Dan's quizzical look, Vic pointed outside. "See the two groups. The women across the street are clearly against the rape of an entire group of women, calling everyone Orion Slave Girls. But, this group right in front of us supports Doster for President. The woman I just passed," he continued in a whisper, "has a sign that says 'Slave Girls for Cookies!' on one side and 'Kill Doster!' on the other."

"That's weird."

"Yeah, see what I mean?" asked Vic.

Dan peered at the woman, but his seat didn't give him the best vantage. "Not quite, but maybe she's bipolar."

"I don't think bipolar would send you to both extremes."

"Probably not. She's still looking outside. I can't see her sign, though."

Vic nodded. "Yeah, it's in the seat next to her."

"She's fiddling with something on the table; not looking at it, just spinning it around and tapping it."

"What is it," Vic asked, his curiosity piqued once more.

Dan craned his neck over the customers in the next booth. "Hell if I know, but it doesn't look normal. I should know. We've got dozens at the travel agency. Looks like a simple brochure for one of the local tourist destinations, maybe the water park or caverns, but it's shining in the sunlight like one of those holographic ball cards."

"Hmmm," mumbled Vic, "is she still staring out the window?"
Dan nodded.

"Something's fishy. I'm no detective, but this doesn't add up."

Smiling at a thought, Dan added, "Maybe she knows something we don't."

"Yeah, like when the next alien invasion will happen," Vic proposed with a laugh, then slunk back into his seat. "Oh, and by the way, thanks for getting me the tickets. You can't control when I get in anyway."

"I know," Dan muttered. "Just wish the timing was better."

*Ba-Bang-Bang.* As the shots rang out, the glass in the far corner of the coffee shop shattered and rained down on the woman they'd just been staring at. The customers leaped from their seats and rushed the glass door.

Through the milieu, Vic glimpsed the woman's devastated face thrust up at the sky. She'd slumped backwards, onto her sign, but the shooter knew what he was aiming at. All three bullets had peppered her face, leaving nothing but blood, gore, and something silver gleaming beneath her skin. It flashed like the brochure had in the sunshine.

"Hoooooly shit!" Vic cried as he dove for the floor. Dan joined him. Rolling out of his chair and pulling his laptop with him, Dan slapped it shut and clutched it to his chest like it were his sole reason for existing.

The crowd's collective panic outside roared into the coffee shop. Shouts and screams rode over the slap of feet on pavement.

Additional shots cracked in the air, and more glass rained onto the shop tables and booths. An amplified voice shouted, "Get on the ground. This is the police. We've cordoned off the area. The wounded will be attended to. You will all be processed and then released."

Vic looked at Dan with questioning eyes. "Processed?"

"That's not the cops. I've got no egg-sucking clue who it is, but it's *so* not the cops."

"Back door, then?" Vic hissed.

"Let's."

The two men crawled toward the counter, Dan using his elbows as he pressed his precious laptop to his chest. Vic glanced to his right. The fearful faces of three coffee-shop patrons stared back at him. He looked at the dead girl, her face ruined by the shots, but her features were beginning to soften. A silver fluid like mercury dripped from her wounds.

The thought occurred that it should have disturbed him more, but aside from its curious nature, it didn't seem that far-fetched.

Once they made it around the counter, they both sat up with their backs to it. Dan looked around for the back exit. Vic turned and saw the girl who'd poured their coffee. She sat wide-eyed, rocking back and forth while hugging her knees.

Vic said, "It's gonna be okay, dearie. Just relax and it'll all be alright."

She nodded absently.

The front door slammed open with a crash, the last jagged shards tumbling to the ground. The sound of glass crunching beneath boots followed. Dan chanced a look through the counter, peering past the doughnuts inside to see what he could. Two men in black fatigues, no insignia, stepped toward one of the prone patrons and ordered, "Look up."

The patron did. One man in fatigues snapped a device at him that flashed. A beep registered, and he said, "Clean. No significant mnemonic contamination."

They stepped to another, a greasy-looking teenage boy that Dan was sure had shown up to the protest to score slave booty.

The device flashed again. "This one's got level-two knowledge of Doster. Authorizing decontamination procedure."

The sound of the shotgun cocking stole the breath of everyone, except the boy.

"Free Doster, you pricks!" he screamed.

A blast of buckshot ensured those were his last words.

Vic looked at Dan, and Dan stared back, beads of sweat appearing on his forehead. He glanced down at his laptop and whispered, "What counts as level two?"

Vic gritted his teeth and looked to the back door. It wasn't far away, but if they tried to make a run for it, they'd be spotted for sure. Maybe if they stayed still, they'd be overlooked.

"Three behind the counter," one of the uniformed men said.

Well, there went that hope.

The pair stepped around the counter, facing Vic, Dan, and the coffee girl. They all three froze.

The device raked harsh light over Vic's eyes. "Negligible contamination."

Dan looked like he might wet himself.

The light came down on Dan's eyes like the judgment of God.

The device emitted an excited, high-pitched alarm. The man holding it said, "My God… it can't be."

The shotgun racked again and the other uniformed man pointed directly toward Dan's face.

"Fuck," the coffee girl said. "I knew this wasn't going to go smoothly."

The two uniforms turned, the weapon and device still pointing at Dan. Surprise flooded their faces at the sight of an apron-clad girl holding a pistol with a silencer as long as her forearm. From the powdered sugar coating it, it must have been stored beneath the Boston Crèmes.

Before anyone could say a word, two muffled shots rang out. The two uniformed men fell dead behind the counter.

Dan looked at her with unvoiced questions, and finally decided on, "What the hell?"

Vic didn't dare speak.

The coffee girl replied, "We're going out the back, now. Come on."

She stayed low, and the men crouched close behind her.

In the back alley she spoke into her wrist, or more specifically, into the thin, rubber bracelet she wore on it. "I have the Principals. Let's get school back in session."

If there was an answer, Dan and Vic couldn't hear it.

They reached the corner panting from the last minute of excitement. In the alley beyond, there was an unmarked white van. The girl turned to stare at Dan. "Seriously… you had to go and look him up on the internet?"

Dan stuttered, "L-lady, I don't know what I've done to piss you off, but if you'll let me go, I'll stop doing it."

She shook her head, "You must have had some intra-personality mask cognitive bleed through. I just hope the unlock code still works."

"What in the living heck are you talking about…?" Dan spat.

The girl interrupted the question with, "Doster's so cool."

"…damn time," Dan said, not dropping a beat. "I was getting claustrophobic in that little mind."

"What the hell's going on here?" Vic shouted.

"Nothing to worry about, sir," Dan intoned. "Just something you did to ensure our survival if we were caught prematurely. Can't have the P-CIA scanning you, now, can we? There isn't time to explain, though. We have to get to launch site two and hook you up to the master mainframe. I'm sure you buried yourself too far for just a simple codeword."

"Am I on the same planet as the two of you?" Vic muttered, his eyes searching for some route of escape.

"You are," the girl answered, a smile quirking the sides of her lips, "and soon you'll be on the one I came from. But not before you and I have a little pre-flight fun to ensure the diversity of my race, big D."

Vic tried unsuccessfully to work through the questions in his mind: what the hell was going on, why his friend and this unusually strong girl were dragging him to the van, and why he wasn't fighting back. In fact, he was only sure of one thing: he was really turned on.

## Considerations

There's something I want you to remember: every madman starts off as just a man. They do the same things that everyone else does. They pay their phone bills. They eat french fries. They find out that the toilet paper roll is empty while they're sitting on the can. Up until the point they stick the knife in or pull the trigger, they're just guys.

I want you to keep that in mind when you hear what I've done.

The day started the same as just about every other one had. I got up. I made coffee, ate a Danish. I drove to work and played online poker while trying to look busy. Then, I went back to my place for lunch.

I came home and something was on the table. It was a bright-red video recorder, one of those new ones that I'd seen ads for that make it look like just owning one will make your life a music video. It had a note on it that said, 'Play me'.

I had no idea who would come into my place and leave mid-grade electronics. I've got friends, but this didn't sound like a prank any of them would pull. I doubted it was the neighbor with my spare key. But there it was.

I wondered if I was on some reality show for a second. I finally said, "Screw it." I picked it up, found the play button, and watched the little screen.

"Hello," a modulated voice said. On the screen was a busload of school kids. The video was shot from the back of the bus. The voice continued, "I want you to see these kids like I found them. I want you to know that I am going to let them laugh and scream and talk about

71

their Hannah Montanas and Spongebobs, and not interrupt their day with mayhem and tragedy.

"That is," the disguised voice continued, "If you do exactly what I tell you. Fail to follow one instruction, and I will make this the worst day of their lives. People will weep all over the country. I will sacrifice them and the dark gods will dance. That is the price of disobedience."

I almost turned it off right there, but I couldn't look away. This was the sickest joke anyone had ever played on me. How had they gotten into the apartment? Somewhere in the back of my head, I became worried that my fingerprints were now on this thing.

"Go to your hall closet," the voice said. "I left you a present. Take it out, unwrap it, then listen to the next instruction. It will be in the bag. See you soon, Brother."

I hit stop and set down the camera. I could have gotten up and called the cops. I could have walked away. I could have ignored it. At least, I thought I could.

But I could feel something in the closet. I could feel the thing that this sick bastard had left for me. I didn't know what it was. I had to know. I got up and went to the closet. I stared at the door, took a deep breath, and opened it.

The closet was almost empty. All my coats were gone except the longest one. Leaning against the wall in the other corner was a duffle bag with a big, red bow on top.

I pulled the bag out, knelt on the floor, gulped, and unzipped it. Inside was something unbelievable. There was a shotgun, the barrel sawed off, a box of shells, and a map of the city. There was also a sword; three feet long with a double edge. All that, and a digital recorder: audio only this time.

"You've taken the first step to true freedom, Brother." The voice was the same as before. "Now, here is what I want you to do."

The instructions still rang in my head as I played the marionette. "Put on the trench-coat and slide the weapons in the pouches we put in the lining." Freedom, true freedom, the voice claimed, but I did none of it by my own volition. I had to save the children. "Go to the coffee shop on the corner of 5th and Beeker, on foot." I trudged the nine blocks. The weight of those lives pressed my shoulders to the ground, my eyes fixed on the sidewalk and shadowed by my foot. Children screamed in excitement as I passed the park. I cringed. My pace quickened of its own accord. Soon, the smells of fresh-ground coffee and baking pastries assaulted my senses back into the moment. "Order a cup and sit down. Place the key to your place on the table and wait."

I didn't have to wait long. A shadow passed my table. I looked up in time to see a tall, thin, Asian man leave the building. I looked back at my table; the key was gone. In its stead were a Bluetooth earbud and a flash drive. I put the ear-piece in and stood. "Be sure to tip your barista, Brother. The bus stop outside, the red line should be there any second. Take it to midtown." The voice sounded so familiar, or was it just that the day was driving his harrowing monotone into my brain? As promised, the red-line doors opened as I exited the building. I fished out my bus pass and headed for a seat in the back. "When you get out at midtown, I want you to head into the bus station. Locker 22, the combination is your birthday: left, right, left. Further instructions await, Brother."

My thoughts drifted, considering the intrusion and how they knew my name until the bus's PA squawked, "Midtown!" I made my way to the front of the bus and down the steps. The sun glared off the glass-covered façade of the Central Records Building. I shielded my eyes, which wandered to the bus station to the right of the CRB, then further to the police station across the street. Again, I contemplated ending this. I started to cross the street, but stopped. Was it guilt or curiosity? I wasn't sure, but I went to the bus station and found my locker. On it was a strange symbol, a peace sign in the shape of an alien head with the four parts of the emblem replaced by a sword, a rifle, a syringe, and strand of DNA. I'd seen the symbol around town and on the news. It had become a fairly popular piece of graffiti, but no group had claimed responsibility. With a bit more trepidation, I reached for the lock. Left 9, Right 22, Left 78… Click!

Another recorder sat there, this time with a map of the CRB.

"Time for your final instructions, Brother. The CRB connects to all government computers. The flash drive in your pocket will free us all if you can get it to the mainframe. That's the X on the map. Your sawed-off has six shots. They have four security guards. Your escape plan is on the roof when you are done. Welcome to freedom. Welcome to the Brotherhood."

Six shots, four guards, what was I doing? Snippets of children flashed by, hooting on a random bus ride home. What if the recording was over, the kids had been dropped off, and they were playing me like a violin? I ran my hand along the stock of the shotgun, checking to be sure it hadn't been a dream. The wood was smooth and polished. It was no dream. The sword's blade gleamed from under the other flap.

Then, the earbud beeped. With a shaky hand, I pressed the receive button and swallow hard.

"Hello again, Brother Maxwell."

"It's Max," I shot back in irritation.

"I know, Brother Maxwell. Thank you for accepting our invitation," replied the tinny voice.

"Did I have a choice?"

"Of course," he replied in his calm tone. "You always have a choice."

"Not much of one."

He harrumphed as though put out, like a child fuming after not getting his way. "Brother Maxwell, you can always turn back. If you aren't willing to continue, I'm sure the children won't mind. It will only hurt the thirty-or-so kids for an instant."

My chest tightened. "How do I know this isn't a trick?"

"It doesn't matter if you believe what I'm saying, Brother. If you want to find out, walk away. I will get what I want. The sacrifice of a busload of children will only bring me the respect and attention I deserve. It's win-win no matter what you choose. But could you live with yourself if you let them die, Brother Maxwell?" The voice paused and let the words sink in.

"No," I croaked.

"Then, time's wasting. The mainframe's in a cooled room in the back. I'll contact you when you've arrived at the room. Stay the course, Brother. Remember, we're watching." The earbud announced the end of the call without waiting for me to respond.

*Dammit, I know you're watching. You don't have to remind me.*

# Strange Circumstances

I pocketed the map and found my way outside, pacing myself as I went so as not to look conspicuous. One-one-thousand, two-one-thousand, three-one-thousand. Kid's lives were at stake. The whole course of events whirled through my head, interrupting my count unbidden. What on earth did the Central Records Building have to do with all of this anyway?

Stepping out from the station, the CRB loomed ahead. I slipped my hands into my coat pockets, holding the heavy flaps closed, and followed the directions.

The bright lobby assaulted my senses with its high ceilings and decoratively tiled floors. A man in a grey suit passed me, stepped through the metal detectors, and flashed his ID at the guard counter before passing into the office of cubicles beyond. The suited man left the lobby vacant, leaving me standing under surveillance cameras and the observation of the guard at the desk. A flurry of office sounds and conversation echoed past the elevators and guard station, into the lobby. Gunfire would alert everyone, and I wouldn't make it far. I caressed the leather handle of the broad sword under my coat. Without an ID or any way to slip past, I'd have to charge upstairs.

My jaw set. I wrapped my hand around the handle and swept through the detectors. They dinged as I tugged the sword free. The Velcro straps gave way and I plunged the blade into the plump, uniformed man's stomach. The man gaped at me, then fumbled at his holster. I slapped my hand over his mouth. Removing his gun, I shoved him into his seat and sliced open his throat. Blood welled onto the floor as he croaked from the office chair, but no words came. I stared in horror. It was too easy, as though taking his life were just a momentary distraction. The sight made me gag, but I didn't have time.

I swallowed the lump in my throat and muttered, "Sorry, but it's the lesser of two evils."

My words were hollow, uncaring. Was I even human? No one should be able to do this and walk away. But I did.

Slipping the sword back under my coat, I crossed a small room with 'Central Records Building' plastered on the wall. The elevator dinged as I pressed the button, and its doors slid open. Two women sauntered out, lost in conversation. I slipped inside, then pressed '10' and the 'Door Close' button. So far, so good. Kenny-G filled the small room as it chimed past each floor. At the sixth floor, the doors opened to admit a balding man in a tie and button-up with a bear claw clenched in one hand. I stepped to the side. He nodded before turning to face the silver doors and taking another bite. Two floors later, the doors opened and he left me alone again. I let out the breath I'd been holding. I could feel my hair turning grey prematurely as the soprano sax wailed from the elevator speakers.

The elevator chimed twice more before revealing a well-lit, windowless hallway. Pictures lined the walls, depicting smiling actors next to supposedly new homes and cars. A guard sat behind a desk at the far end. He glanced up from his book, folded the top of one page, and set it down.

"Hey, can I help you?" he asked as I neared.

My mouth was sealed as though a gob of peanut butter had cemented my tongue to the roof of my mouth.

"Can I help you find something?" he repeated, gripping his sidearm cautiously.

# Strange Circumstances

I fiddled with the sword beneath my jacket as though searching for something. "N-n-no," I stammered. "I've got my pass right here."

The guard watched with curiosity while I dug inside my jacket. With my other hand, I aimed the other guard's handgun in my large coat pocket and fired. The trigger clicked over and over beneath my finger, hammering bullets into the man's chest until the gun gave a hollow click. After six shots, the uniformed man staggered into the wall groaning, but removed his gun while wavering in place.

I recoiled in horror as the man grinned painfully and raised his weapon. I dodged to the side as the gun echoed in the hallway. Bullets ricocheted off the floor, into walls and glass pictures. The sword flew from my coat and swept down on his extended arm without thought. An upward swing split his groin. The man screamed for a split-second before the third stroke severed his head. The body fell to the ground with two gurgling thumps.

That someone could take so many shots and still remained standing was incredible. I stared at the bloody chaos and stifled a feeling of nausea. "The lesser of two evils. Gotta save the kids," I mumbled to the blood-spattered room.

A white, metal door stood behind the desk with a card reader mounted on the wall. I tried the door, but it held firm. Just then a siren wailed.

Okay, two down, two to go. There was no time to waste. I retrieved the guard's ID from his tattered shirt, wiped the blood away, and slid it through the scanner. A locking mechanism released inside the wall, and I passed through. A room filled with computers greeted me.

"What are you doing here?" inquired a slender woman in a blouse and black miniskirt. Spotting the bloody sword, she yelped and dove under a table.

I ignored her, opened an inner door, and left the woman behind. Next-door was a larger room filled with computer-laden tables and cubicles. A host of people sat at each terminal, typing away. They were so focused only a few noticed me enter, but their screams alerted the others. I swept past, toward a door at the far end of the hall. But before I reached it, the office door admitted two more security guards with drawn pistols. The screams seemed to fade away as the men confronted me. I was running out of time. My instincts shouted to stop, but instead I panicked. I charged, leaped onto a table scattering computer mice and keyboards, then hurled myself at the men. Gunfire exploded ahead of me, and something splintered my forearm before I collided with the men. We went down in a tangled heap of bodies and weapons.

Unsure where the sword had disappeared, I kicked away and pulled the shotgun from its sheath. One man stopped fumbling for his gun and held up his hands. The other was searching the floor.

"Sorry, I don't have time for you." I pulled the trigger and sent the man staggering backward, then exercised its pump-action loading and turned it on his partner. The gunshot had gotten his attention, and his eyes pleaded with me. I closed mine and pulled the trigger, pumped it again, and fired once more. Pictures shattered and fell in a cacophony of sound. When I looked at the carnage, two haggard bodies lay crumpled on the navy-blue carpet. My heart went out to them and their families. The grief was almost overwhelming. The officer's pleading face appeared in my mind. I shuddered.

"The lesser of two evils," I reminded myself. I wiped tears from my cheek. "They're going to pay. Somehow, they will." I chambered another shell, and slipped through the door, my eyes darting everywhere.

I entered a vacant room with a desk, two chairs, and walkie-talkies blaring in their chargers. "Intruder on level ten," squawked a voice. "James, you there? Level ten, can you hear me? What's your situation?"

A second, deeper voice responded. "Mays, I've got him on camera in the level ten security room. He's packing and covered in blood."

"Is he dead?" shouted Mays.

"Nah, he's actually looking at the camera. I'm not sure what happened to James and Casey, but it don't look so good."

I crossed the small room and grabbed a walkie, wincing at the painful twinge in my arm. They're watching my every move. I had to get out of that room. Using the security ID, I passed into the next room. A gust of cool air tickled my skin. Racks of computer servers were mounted in rows. Setting the walkie down, I locked the door and lodged a chair back under the knob. Then, I removed the map from my pocket and double-checked my location. This was the place.

"He just passed into the server room," squawked the handheld. The earbud chimed.

"Brother Maxwell, I see you've found your way," whispered the man.

"Yeah, so turn off the bomb."

"In time. Brother, find the computer server labeled 'Host 1'."

The aisles of shelves flew by as I scanned each one. On the far end, next to a large window spanning the wall, I came across 'Host 1'. "Yeah, what now?"

"Simple, Brother Maxwell," he whispered, "insert the flash drive into a USB slot and watch the magic."

"It's Max," I retorted once more, reaching for the port. My hand wavered in front of it. "But how do I know you'll let the kids go?"

"You'll have to trust me, but if you walk away now, it was all for noth…"

"Steven, don't do this?" interrupted a condemning voice in the background.

Something rubbed against the receiver, muffling the connection. Steven's stifled voice yelled, "I told you to be quiet. Now zip it!"

"Steven, Steven Essex?" I asked. The flash drive fell from my hands at the revelation, tumbling onto the carpet.

Steven cleared his throat. "Uh, no."

"Yes it is. I recognize your voice now."

"Dammit, Max, just do what you're told," he demanded.

Memories of the few times we'd met came to mind. We were half-brothers, but he had just been born when I left for college. I hadn't seen him much after that. The thought depressed me, and I picked up the pocket drive. "Steven, what the hell are you doing? Aren't you supposed to be at college?"

"Jesus, can't you do one simple thing, Max?"

"You organized this? I murdered people, Steven. There isn't a busload of kids, is there?" My stomach twisted in knots.

Steven hissed, "No, there isn't. Just do this. Put the drive into the computer."

"What's this about? I-I can't believe you did this."

"Nah, I didn't do this. You did. Are you scared yet?"

"Steven, I c-can't believe you did this." My knees loosened as though the joints had been doused with grease. They threatened to give way at any moment.

"Whatever. Either way, you're screwed," he replied. "Just plug the damn drive in."

I didn't answer. A moment later his tone changed. "You've gotta do it. I've never asked you for anything."

I peered down at the port. Shame stabilized my legs and tried to settle the panic raging inside my chest. I'd just killed four people. The doorknob squeaked as it tried to turn. The lock rattled open, but the door jarred on the chair. Someone began pounding on it, screaming, "There's no way out. Just give up."

"Brother Maxwell," interrupted Steven.

"Quit calling me that," I snapped. "I'll do it."

I slid the drive into the port, and a digital window opened on the flat-screen monitor strapped above. 'Connecting' it said. A moment later a live video popped up. Steven waved at me from a living room, a young man in his mid-twenties wearing a burgundy polo, slacks, and the innocent smile I remembered from his childhood. It couldn't have belonged to someone that would mastermind such a gruesome act. But the gleam in his eyes said differently.

"Hello, Brother. Welcome to my world."

"Why?" was the only word that came to mind.

"Why, oh, that's so cliché. For research, of course. Are you afraid? Do you regret killing those people?"

"Steven, stop it!" shouted an older man. The voice that had interrupted earlier belonged to a man bound to a rustic, dining-room chair, his arms disappearing from view behind his back. A mop of tousled gray hair contrasted with his checkered vest and khakis.

"Stop it? But this is the best part. What was it you said in class?" Steven tapped his chin, then mimicked the man's professorial voice quite well. "Oh yeah, 'It's almost impossible to determine the cause of psychotic breaks and rampaging lunatics.' Now, we can." If it were possible, his grin widened with self-satisfaction.

The older gentleman groaned, and his head dropped shamefully to his chest.

"Steven, what are you talking about?" I asked. "Why did you do this?"

"Isn't it obvious? To see what it would take to send a normal person to the brink, to motivate someone to kill. Brother Maxwell," he continued with detached superiority, "welcome to my graduate thesis, *Fear as a Motivation for Murder*."

My stomach did a somersault this time, struggling to find some route of escape while more fists and bodies began pounding on the server room door. "Oh, God, what have I done?" The security guard's pleading eyes returned, haunting me from just out of sight.

"Just what was needed," answered Steven.

The professor mumbled, "None of this was necessary, Steven. You need help. Please, untie me."

"Not necessary? But, Mr. Krylech, now we have proof, undeniable evidence of what will drive a man to murder. Anyone can

blackmail someone into it. Fear is our primary human weakness."
Steven's voice continued, his words melding together as he debated
the issue with Mr. Krylech. They became a jumbled buzzing in my ear.

It couldn't be true, not really. I'd killed... murdered those
men. They were doing their jobs, had families at home... I slaughtered
them. I fondled the sawed-off shotgun, running my fingers over its
murderous handle. Flipping the weapon around, I positioned my
thumb over the trigger. The taste of metal alloy leaked onto my tongue
from the barrel. Resting my teeth on its hard, slick surface, I pulled the
trigger. The gun exploded, and there was a moment of sharp, intense
pain. The buzzing voices stopped, and everything vanished in a
blanket of night.

* * * * *

"So you see, Saint Peter, I belong here." I wave a hand at the
gleaming gate and cloudy expanse beyond. "It wasn't my fault. Don't
turn me away."

A bearded man sits before me with crossed legs, a brown robe,
and sandals. He could have been Moses's brother. He might be. I
never kept up with religion or even read the Bible, something I'm
beginning to regret. "I understand," says the grandfatherly man, his
gentle, knowing eyes weighing my words.

I squirm, repositioning myself on the large rock
uncomfortably. Who would have thought the entrance to Heaven
would be so barren? A black asphalt road leads to the gate, the tar
sticky as though the avenue were newly made. Two large rocks act as
temporary seats, one for me, and the other for Saint Peter. He seems at

home, listening but saying little. A puffy expanse of desert clouds makes up the entire world as far as I can see. It's as though we are all that exists.

Saint Peter scratches his chin, then smooths some straggling hairs back down. After what feels like an eternal pause, he mutters, "Hmmmm… what to do with you?"

## Sandmen

The Thrice Rubbed Lamp was the only bar in town open at 6:00 a.m. Technically, their hours were 6:00 p.m. until noon the following day. They had to acquire the status of "Private Club" to keep such hours, but it had paid off. Their customers were good tippers and thirsty drinkers, all of whom kept odd hours, and many were regulars.

Among them were Harry, Olaf and Dwight. They were the three busiest sandmen in town. They had three chairs that the bartender, Hortence, kept open for them.

On this particular day, it was Harry that arrived last. His shoulders drooped and he dragged his leather boots along the floor as he walked. Olaf and Dwight both felt him come in and turned to watch as he drug himself into the chair that, over the years, had taken on the exact contours of his rear end.

Harry barely got his bag of sand onto the bar and raised his hand to request his usual Piña Colada before Olaf asked, "What the hell happened to you?"

Harry straightened in his chair with a small effort before Hortence slid him his usually umbrella-adorned beverage. Harry took a sip and said, "I'd suggest you not ask…"

"Too late," Dwight replied, sipping his Heineken. Dwight always got the same drink, too, and always from a can, never a bottle.

"…except that," Harry continued, his eyes now narrowed in contempt at his colleague.

"Rough night, then" Olaf interjected. He had yet to drink from his vodka tonic. Instead, he swirled the ice around the glass with the little straw that no one's ever sure whether or not to sip from.

"Yeah," Harry said. He took another long pull on his straw and said. "A doozy."

"Well," Dwight prompted, leaning forward. "Spill it. Wet dream? Nightmare? Wet Nightmare?"

"Oh, worse," Harry continued. "This one was lucid. I'm trying to help him untwist his subconscious, and here he is trying to take back the steering wheel."

Olaf interrupted, "We don't really steer so much as suggest, Harry...."

Harry jumped in and said, "Actually, I was being literal. I was chauffeuring him around some amusement park, helping him get over some pants-wetting thing, when he jumped in the front seat and tried to steer. I had to do some fancy footwork."

Harry took another drink. Olaf looked at Dwight and raised an eyebrow. Dwight said, "Go on, then."

"I followed protocol. I let him think I was just some odd version of himself, and I gently tried to suggest he wasn't dreaming and that he just should just go with it, but he got all insistent and tried to make the car fly. I swear! It was all I could do to try to keep him from falling out of the dream."

"Maybe you should have let him," Olaf harrumphed.

"I've worked with this dreamer for a long time," Harry mumbled, brushing earwax off his shoulder from where he'd exited the dreamer's mind. "He's got a lot of shame to shake off. I'm really close to a good thirty percent boost in self confidence and self esteem."

"Shooting for bonus this month, huh?" Dwight asked.

"Just doing my job," Harry replied. "Not that you'd know anything about that."

Dwight turned, his eyes wide. "That's a hell of a thing for you to say. Besides, I'll have you know that my night was pretty flawed too. May have even been worse than yours."

"What?" Harry and Olaf asked in a jumble, brows knitted.

"My dreamer went lucid, too," Dwight added. He glared at his drink and took a long pull of his Heineken, shook the empty can at the bartender, and then set it on the far side of the bar. He said, "Let me tell you about it."

"Oh," Olaf muttered with an anxious glint in his eyes, "I want to hear this one."

Dwight took the new can and popped the top with a sigh. "Barbara's been at a loss since that rape I told you about last year."

"You can't still be trying to fix that girl," Olaf spat. "I thought you would've dropped her by now, bonus or not."

Dwight ignored him. "She could hardly walk into a supermarket without panicking and running back to her car. Deathly afraid of people and their unpredictability."

At the mention of Barbara's rape, Hortence began listening curiously while pouring other customer's drinks. "How did you wind up with that little morsel anyway?"

"Little morsel?" inquired Dwight in a whisper, as though suddenly aware of Barbara's looks. "Well, she changed a bit. She wasn't as lean as she was in the papers when her last movie came out. She lost a lot of weight and was practically skin and bones. Did you check out the latest Sandsy Times?"

The others shook their heads. "Nah, there's no reason to read about what other Sandmen are doing. I've got my hands full with my assignments," Harry muttered.

"Well, they had a picture of Barbara in it, a recent one," Dwight continued. "Man, just thinking about her puts knots in my stomach. I couldn't drop her. I had to help, no matter how hard it was. This time, she pulled in someone else. They had their own dream keeper; Marcus, you know him?"

"Yeah," added Hortence. "He comes in every third day, sits in the far corner."

Dwight nodded, "He won't anymore. I was taking Barb through the final steps of phase three, acquainting her with the past and all. We'd just visited her family and others that had gone through similar situations, and she started seizin' like you wouldn't believe. We were deep in her subconscious and had just appeared in Stanley's old mansion, her attacker. We hadn't even found him yet, but the place was enough. I thought we'd stumbled on a trigger, some connection to the place I hadn't fully investigated. The rape hadn't happened there, but something set her off. Then, in comes a scythe-wielding banshee crashing through the large stained-glass window high in the ceiling. The cretin had to have been twelve feet tall when it landed on the staircase and dropped Marcus's head to the ornate tile below."

"Whoa, hold on. Where'd that come from?" asked Olaf in rapt attention.

"Well, I'm not sure, but on its back was some young boy, couldn't have been more than eight years old. He was smacking the banshee in the back of the head, but the effort hardly disturbed the creature's waves of hair, let alone distracted it. The kid must've been

Marcus's charge. The tyke wasn't running or anything, so Marcus had done a bang-up job helping him overcome whatever was eating at him, but they obviously hadn't reached level five. The kid didn't know how to control it, and somehow Barbara's panic must've let the boy's nightmare into her dream."

"I've never heard of a connection like that," interrupted Olaf.

"Me either," added Hortence from across the bar. The bartender was polishing the same glass he'd been working on for the last few minutes as he listened in.

"Surprised me, too. The banshee swooped down at us with the boy struggling on its back. But bless her heart, Barbara straightened up and shoved me aside, seizing control of the dream. I flew across the floor and into a coat closet. Her thin frame shimmered as she went lucid, facing the plunging demon and literally pulling the house down on top of us. The banshee was crushed under the falling ceiling and large chandelier. Then, everything came down. All that was left was dust."

"So, is she still alive? Is she still your charge?" asked Harry.

"I'm afraid not. When she died in the dream, she never woke up. I'd feel her subconscious, but it's as though it vanished. So, I'm sure they'll assign me someone new tonight." The mention of his lost charge lowered Dwight's head into his beer.

Olaf asked tentatively, "So, even Marcus lost control of the dream?"

"Appears so," Dwight mumbled after a large swig.

"That's insane. How could an eight-year-old summon something like that?" asked Olaf.

"Must've been one hell of a nightmare. Don't know what happened the day before, but something rattled him," answered Dwight.

Harry had remained quiet, but now whispered, "It might have something to do with my charge." Harry's Piña Colada disappeared down his throat in one gulp. The familiar wince of a man with brain-freeze slid across his face as he signaled Hortence for another.

Dwight stared on his own drink, and Olaf slid to the edge of his seat. "Out with it, man! Don't leave us hanging like that."

Harry drew in a breath and looked at his rapt audience. "My dreamer's dying." A quick sip from his refreshed drink, and he continued, "We were literally driving down memory lane when he took the wheel. I was trying to push him toward acceptance."

"Hence the confidence and self-esteem work," whispered Dwight.

"Right. Well, halfway through the park where I had his regrets laid out he went lucid and decided he needed redemption instead of acceptance." Harry coughed, seemingly embarrassed, before going on in a more strained tone. "This guy was a hard case and a long time abuser of himself and everyone else. I should have killed the dream, but I needed the bonus. Thirty percent for acceptance is good, but I needed the hundred percent for reform. Margaret and I are broke. We might lose the house, so I let the car fly straight toward his demons."

Olaf shook his head. "You married a tooth fairy. How are you guys broke?"

Dwight set his hand on Olaf's shoulder. "Let him finish."

Another long pull from his drink and Harry went on. "When most people confront their demons, they are metaphorical. I know he used to sexually abuse his son, so we headed to Stanley's Mansion."

"Wait! Was your charge Barbara's rapist?"

"No, Olaf, Marcus's was. The eight-year-old boy was Stanley confronting his issues with his father. He dreamed him the way he always did: tall, dark, and impossibly strong. Because of their past and us coming to the same place in the dream, the dreams merged. Stanley's father became one with Stanley's nightmare. I lost control. The dream collapsed, and I ran."

Dwight stood up and put a hand on Harry's arm. "Why were you so late then?"

Tears cut runnels of mud through the dream sand on Harry's face. "I got fired. They're blaming me for Marcus's death and a renegade nightmare on the loose. They merged so completely that his body disappeared from the nursing home."

*Clap, clap, clap*, came the sound of rough hands from the far end of the bar.

"You missed your calling, dream-weaver. You are an excellent storyteller. I wanted to thank you in person for allowing me to fix my mistake. I was too soft on the boy all those years." The shadow in the corner unfolded and stood at an impossible height. A scythe that would make Death proud formed in his hand. As he raised the blade high, he whispered through a maniacal grin, "No witnesses!"

## Ding

The sweat on my lips tastes salty, and all the teeth on the right side of my mouth feel like they're ready to abandon ship. The crowd's cheers and boos are a dull roar in my ears, though I can't tell anymore which sounds are intended for me and which are for him. My lungs are on fire and my thighs want to seize like an engine 2000 miles overdue for an oil change.

And… it's only Round Three.

The kid is good. Jeremy tried to warn me before I stepped into the ring, but I had to prove him wrong. I tried to treat it just like any other fight; two guys walking in upright and just me walking out on my feet. But that was how I thought the last two would go, and they didn't work out exactly as planned.

I shift my feet, feint right, and then go right again to throw a left jab. But the kid doesn't go for it. I turn my eyes enough to see his left hand coming, an uppercut I can't afford to take, even if I hadn't just stepped into it.

The whole world slows down. Every detail is in sharp focus: the beads of sweat on his face, the look of horror one of the announcers has as he sees what's about to happen, the lady in the third row spilling her longneck beer as she gestures for the kid to take my damn head off.

And that's when I see him. He's not the ref. He's not the announcer. And where everything else is moving like molasses, he's stepping up to me like a waiter who wants to check on his customer.

I move my eyes back to the kid. He's not reacting to him. I look to the announcers. They don't see him. And I wonder, maybe, if I've taken one too many shots to the dome.

The guy speaks up. "Bryce, you're not dreaming. You're really seeing me. I know you're busy, but it really couldn't wait."

I look down. The punch is coming and I can't do anything about it, but it's not going to get here for a while. "Do I know you?" I ask.

"In a manner of speaking. But it's not important. What is important is why you want to win this fight."

"Alright then, who are you?"

He straightens his paisley-print tie, flicks a piece of lint off of his suit's lapel, and then says, "Think of me as a trainer for a fight you didn't know was coming."

"Okay," I say. "Not to be a jerk here, but could we do this another time? I'm in the middle of something."

He smiles and I feel my kegels tighten. "I assure you, this is worth your time, Bryce. But before we go further, there's something you should take a look at."

He snaps his fingers and vanishes. I start to turn and look for him, but things speed up to normal. My opponent's glove instantly jacks my jaw and a sky's worth of twinkling stars appear above, but I know I'm not going down... When my eyes finally regain their focus, I'm not in the ring anymore.

I'm sitting in the house we used to rent on West High Street with algebra homework in front me on the kitchen table. My mom and dad are fighting. I'm trying to ignore it as best as a high-school kid can.

But then Dad does something he never did before. Mom pulls a hand up to her slack-jawed face because she can't believe it, even though she can still feel the sting. I am across the room before I realize it, pulling my hand back to throw a haymaker, the kind coach has been telling me since I was twelve to never throw because they see it coming.

Dad doesn't see it coming.

I feel the contact and hear the crowd erupt. The kid stumbles back and I push forward to throw a left hook. Then, things slow again.

From beside me, Mr. Paisley-Tie whispers, "Good punch. Now... where were we? Or more importantly, where will you be next?" Then, he disappears.

The kid's jab slices through the arc of my hook in time for me to catch it square in the nose. My hand comes away bloody, and I'm instantly standing in the alley behind my childhood arcade. The guy holding me is Jimmy Richardson: a pipsqueak and toady. The one that just gifted me the first of many broken noses is Mitchell Montgomery. I twist out of Jimmy's grip and a punch glances past my cheek. I turn into the punch and catch Mitch in the ear.

The crowd is more boos than cheers now as the ref pulls me away from the kid. He's lying in a heap at my feet, and my head's still ringing from his uppercut. Then things get slow again, so I try to take advantage. "You know, I really despise paisley. Why would anyone willingly wear it?"

"Here I thought I was preparing a fighter, not a fashion critic." That high laugh tells me he isn't giving up anything yet. "Your cut man is good. You met him in the Army, right?"

# Strange Circumstances

The world speeds back up. Water sloshes over my head and face as my cut man stitches up my chin. The crowd noises blend, as do the pictures of Arnie as he is now and when he was Sgt. Bilkes. "Good to see you in uniform again, Sarge." The smelling salts pull me back to reality and Arnie back into his sweats.

"Kid must'a hit ya harder than I thought, Bryce. Neither of you will make it through the fourth at the rate you're going. Finish him fast."

"'Kay, Sarge."

"We need to speed this up." The suit's voice is unctuous. It slides through my consciousness like an oiled snake. "Why don't I let you wander a bit and see where that takes us?"

I don't know what exactly he means, but I do know the ring girl as she walks by with the card for round four. When she turns one way, she's Betty, my ex-wife. When she turns another, she's Jessica, the reason Betty left. All the while, she's still Celia, the ring girl that shot me down as too old less than an hour ago. The kid across the ring is Mitchell, my Father, the Marine that almost ended my career, and finally me before settling back into the twenty-four-year-old powerhouse that's pushed me past my limit today. The ring ropes change from red to blue, then to actual rope. It's like I'm fighting every adversary I've ever faced at once, and the bell just rang.

I stand. His gloves are shifting beneath my gaze too. A feint, and the kid flashes his left toward my ribs. I know that move. He's the Marine. I block high and counter with an uppercut, letting the useless rib shot land. He almost killed me with that move once. He did get me discharged from the Army. Now, he's trying to use his height advantage, just like dear old Dad. It's a disadvantage too, if you can't use it well. I ball up, get inside his reach and punish his ribs. He pushes me away. He's Mitchell Montgomery trying to use his strength to overpower me, but it's undisciplined, desperate. He leaves me large openings to punish him. I don't care what time I'm in or who I'm fighting anymore. The crowd is all cheers as my last punch lands on the kid's jaw and he launches into the air. Time crawls again. The fall to the mat is taking an eternity.

*Clap. Clap. Clap.* "Well done. I think that worked perfectly. You are, indeed, the man I was told you could be." He turns and opens a door in the center of the ring that wasn't there before. "You can call me Mr. Johnson. If you'll follow me, I have a job for you."

Shouts and catcalls echo throughout the auditorium as time returns to normal. After counting down the seconds with an extended hand, the ref shouts T.K.O. and raises my wrist into the air. The knowledge of what is to come forces my smile to falter. Another match… another fighter… and I would lose. The paisley man is my key to success. The half-wit would have pummeled me if Mr. Johnson hadn't done what he did… but what did he do?

Slipping out of the ref's grip, I walk toward the door. In my final steps, the cheering ground slumbers as though someone hit the mute button. My eyes hone in on the door, and I fight the urge to look around. There's nothing left for me here. As I step through the white light encasing the doorway, everything slips into its proper speed, but where am I?

Mr. Johnson's leaning on a line of extra-large lockers. The pale green of the metal is reminiscent of the service lockers in the Army, but even they weren't this big. The man could live in one of them. For all I know, he does. Above them, rusting televisions line the high ceiling, broadcasting a million different lives at once.

"Hello, Bryce," he whispers with a smile and flicks another speck of lint from his tie.

"Happy to see me?" I ask.

"Of course, but I knew you'd come along. A great fighter always leaves at the peak of his career."

"The peak? It's a little late for that, but that fight should get people talking." The room is dank and humid. My hands are drowning in their gloves after such an adrenaline rush, but his voice keeps my attention.

"Yes, it will," Mr. Paisley Tie answers with a nod. "And it's a good thing too. You're right. Your career was past its prime, as are you."

Hearing it said so nonchalantly is depressing, but he's right.

"Really, your life was pretty much over."

"Wait." I wave my hands to focus his eyes. For some reason, they'd drifted to the floor. "My life wasn't over. I ain't that old. It's just a career."

"It's your life; everything you've done since your good-ol' dad was sent off to the Pen. And you had a choice: Army or prison. The only thing you're good at is fighting. That's what they trained you for. Don't deny it. You... quit boxing?" Mr. Johnson gave a hearty laugh. "Right!"

My eyes drift to the shadowed cement floor. The bulbs hanging high overhead sway in the enclosed room, making the shadows shift under my gaze. Aching for something to do, I tear at my taped wrists with my teeth like a wolf caught in a bear trap. I've had to do it on my own plenty since the money stopped flowing. After losing so many bouts, I had to let most of my staff go… everyone but Sarge. He isn't in it for the money. But it's over now.

"Here, let me get that," mumbles Mr. Johnson. Pushing himself off the lockers, he relieves me of the gloves. "You're gonna need something a bit heavier in a minute. These just won't do."

"Wait… in a minute? What are you jabberin' about?"

"Like I said before, I've got a job for you," he replies, setting the gloves on a large table. Something scrapes the metal table's surface as he turns to me. He holds aloft two corroded gloves with interlinked armor plates around each finger and chain webbing over the hands. "These will do nicely."

"What? What the hell are you talking about? I ain't puttin' those on. They can't even work in that condition."

"What did you think my job would be? As I said, you come highly recommended. You'll do fine, and these work perfectly well."

"Do fine at what? Recommended by who?" I shout. "What are you talking about?"

"Come now," Mr. Johnson tsks, stepping forward. "By crossing into this world, you accepted the job. We need you, and there's no way back."

Glancing back, enormous green lockers line the wall. There's nothing left of the doorway. I try one, but it doesn't budge. What is it… magic?

"Like I said, there's no way back." He nods at the lockers. "Only us Searchers have the combination to those. You admitted that your life was over. Here, you can begin anew and be our savior. You've got to win. That's your only hope, and ours." The rusted links of the chain gloves flex in his hands, the metal plating tapping together as though counting down the seconds until Mr. Paisley Tie's appointed minute is up.

"But who recommended me? What's all this?" I ask with a wave of my hand.

Mr. Johnson stiffens, his back straight as a street lamp. "Look, we watch for the best people to come to our rescue. It's our job as Searchers. You're our last hope. So please, put these on."

Seeing no option, I flex my fingers, crack my knuckles, and hold my palms out to be fitted.

\* \* \* \* \*

The tunnel out to the ring smells like rotting corpses. Furry rodents with floppy ears too large for a rabbit speed by as though fleeing the light at the end of the passageway, some with gnawed bones jutting from behind their yellow buck teeth.

"Who am I facing?" I ask, flexing my gauntleted fingers.

"A monster, the chosen gladiator of the King. She's never been beaten, until now. But remember, don't run when you get out there or the guards'll nail you to the pavement like a pin-cushion."

Suddenly, our solitary footsteps seem much louder. I peer back down the rotting passage and swallow the frog attempting to crawl up my throat. Too late to do a damn thing about it now. "And why did you pick me again? I'm over the hill. You said it yourself. Why did you even need me to finish that match?"

"To see if you had it in you to best the unbeaten," Mr. Paisley Tie replies, but his eyes remain focused on the light at the end of the tunnel. A chanting roar begins to echo toward us.

"What's her name?"

"I can't say," he answers.

"Can't or won't?"

"Can't... don't know their language. They just call her Meg'arum."

"They?"

"Yeah, the fans. Now listen, look out for her arms."

"Why her arms?" I ask as we step into the light.

"Because she's got four of 'em."

To emphasize his point, the tunnel opens onto the edge of a large crater ringed by stalagmites the size of mountains. Seeing me, a muscle-bound Amazonian with ragged braids of hair roars from the center of the ring, her scarred arms flung high as though directing the audience's cries with her spears. Even at this distance, patches of coarse, dark hair staining her arms are visible. A large cord hangs around her broad neck, decorated with bleached skulls that look miniscule compared to her own.

"Whoa, where'd they find her? And don't tell me those are real skulls."

"On a world you don't want to visit, and don't ask questions you don't want the answers to," Mr. Johnson replies.

I force down the overwhelming nausea erupting in my stomach. This is it. It's the only way. I have to win. I can do this. Johnson picked me for a reason...

"Wait a sec…," I whisper, "why'd you pick me? Why not Tyson or some heavyweight celebrity?"

Mr. Paisley Tie quirked an eyebrow but finally looked me in the eyes. "How likely is one of them to leave the profession? Come on kid, use your noggin."

"Right… right. You sure I don't get a bit more armor? This doesn't look too fair."

"Fair," Mr. Johnson blurts with a laugh. "This isn't supposed to be fair, kid. We've been searching for a champion that can best Meg'arum for eons. Sheesh… fair. Was it fair when the Horats invaded our world, taking it for their own and forcing us to live off scraps? Why do you think I've been looking for just the right person? If we win, we have a chance."

Flushed with shame, I nod and avoid his eyes. "Let's get on with it."

Mr. Johnson leads me down a meandering path, through the crowded audience, and into the circular basin. At the edge of the crowd, a man with a bullhorn shouts, "And we have our latest selection. Bryce Wilcox will attempt to slay the mighty Meg'arum. Step forward, Bryce, and try not to piss yourself."

A roar of laughter echoes from the crowd, much like the jeering mass on my world, only ten times larger. The sounds resound up the stalagmites ringing the enormous crater like the lingering memories of a haunted house. "Well, wish me luck," I mumble, clenching my armored hands nervously. "I'll do my best."

"I'm sure you will." A sly smile tweaks the edges of his lips, and his tie flutters in the currents as a gust whips through the towers of rock. His shoulders shake with an escalating chuckle; then Mr. Paisley

Tie lets out a boisterous laugh. "Remember, don't run. Just try to last long enough to double my money." Flicking his hand, he turns to a pudgy man in the audience.

"Great Job, Johnson. Twenty ingles is your finder's fee."

I can't see Johnson's face, but his distressed tone says it all. "But, Mr. Clark, that can't be right. This is my fortieth find."

"It's what you get," answers the rotund man. "Do ya want it or not?"

Mr. Paisley Tie nods and takes a wad of Monopoly money. Forty people? How many Searchers are there? Meg'arum's giant face looms nearer as I step into the crater's center. Even at forty paces, it's huge. The bleached skulls clink around her neck at eye level. She's killed god knows how many people, and I'm next. The lump in my throat returns with a vengeance, but a growing rage makes it a dwindling concern. That bastard picked me as bait: something to pay the bills. Everything else was a lie.

"And they're off," blares the bull horn as though this is a horse race. A second later, Meg'arum leaps forward like a banshee on stilts, closing the distance in an instant. Fear grips my stomach, pushing all thoughts from my mind. I turn and bolt for the exit, but the audience has closed it off, jeering as the behemoth barrels down on me. I have to keep my distance. I curve around the crater, trying not to lose my pace. But a quick glance back shows the futility of such an attempt. Meg'arum's gaining, the ground beneath us dwindling with each tremendous step.

"You simple bitch! Can't you do anything right?" echoes my father's voice as my mother sits crying at the table next to me. The world doesn't slow, but I know the memory. It's from earlier than the

103

one I had in the ring. The large man didn't care about us. We were smaller and weaker than him.

My pace begins to falter, and I peer back at Meg'arum once more. The similar chiseled jaw and coal-black eyes are undeniable. My fists clench and I spin, duck her spear, and throw myself into her knees. She stumbles, pitches forward, and plummets into the well-trodden dirt of the crater floor.

Try to last long enough. Hell, I've beaten worse... I think.

I leap onto her back, planting a knee in her spine, and pummeling the back and sides of her head mercilessly. The metal gauntlets catch in her long, ragged hair and tear strips of flesh from her scalp. Blood flies through the air and Mitchell lies below me on the alley pavement.

"Stop, stop... please stop..." he whimpers, but his cries turn to vicious grunts. He melts away, leaving Meg'arum to push herself up and backhand me across the dirt floor.

Stars blaze to life yet again, checkering my vision as the horrid giant steps up with a snarl. She sets a large, calloused foot on my bare chest. My ribs creak. Raising a spear overhead, she thrusts it down. The jagged point slices through the stars and into my shoulder as I roll left, pushing her foot away and twisting with all my might. She might have four arms, but she still needs both legs. Meg'arum topples and falls like she's the Jolly Green Giant stepping in a fox hole. Seizing the moment, I tenderize her Achilles' heel, shredding the skin with my armored knuckles.

Before she can rise again, I leap to my feet and dance away, flinching from the spear tip grinding against my shoulder bone as it falls to the floor. I shove the pain aside, locking it deep within me.

A grin splits my face as Meg'arum flashes to my father rising after my hay-maker sent him to the ground. When she looks up, her dark eyes are those of my last successful defeat... before Mr. Paisley Tie entered my life... back when fighting made sense; my last true success in the ring, my peak some might say. Domingo Velasquez's eyes blazed with hatred, but something else had entered them... the fear of defeat. Velasquez disappears and Meg'arum's eyes are the same. She isn't finished, but I'd surprised her. Meg'arum steps forward, favoring her bad foot.

A smarter man might wait, but I can't stop the energy flowing through my body. Every inch of me is taut. My muscles tingle, aching for more... for the taste of victory. I can do more than last, Mr. Johnson. I'm gonna kick her ass.

Time speeds up. My muscles clench, twist, and tense as my fists smash into her fleshy face. Her arms wrap around me and lift me off my feet, her spears lost under the deluge of blows. She squeezes, and my bones crack, but it's like some noise in the distance, echoing off the spired crater walls. Her bloody, train-wrecked face glares at me, somehow pleading through the daggers glistening in her eyes. But the high is euphoric.

My gauntlets rattle her head, blow after blow, and I slam my elbows into her enormous skull. The giant Amazonian gnashes her teeth, ripping at my exposed chest and stomach like a rabid wolverine, but the pain belongs to someone else.

Her eye sockets groan under the beating and one side of her face slackens. I don't stop. I can't. Minutes pass in seconds. There's little left of her nose. Her eyes are blood-shot and losing focus. Her arms slacken and her head slumps back, exposing itself to the heavens

105

and me. Anxious excitement courses through me, and I hammer her revealed face, reveling as the skin and body parts are ripped away. Meg'arum unconsciously lowers me to the ground as she wavers in place. My grin widens. Her ribs are exposed and my clenched hands tickle them with a rapid vigor I've never known.

Then, the ancient tree falls. A thunderous boom echoes through the silent, make-shift stadium as the onlookers gawk at the havoc I wrought on their champion. Time returns to normal, and suddenly, flashes of pain sear my brain, branding it like cattle. The effort to stand is too much, and I slump to the ground and cradle my head in my sticky, metal hands.

"Wilcox," yells a small voice from the back of the stadium. Somehow, it breaches the flaming thoughts, working its way to my consciousness. "Wilcox... Wilcox... Wilcox..." The audience begins to take up the chant. The name reverberates across the inverted dome, echoing off others' lips.

A rough hand grips my shoulder and jerks me to my feet. I will my anguish aside once more and level cold eyes on the speaker. The euphoric high is gone.

"Can I go home now?" I ask through gritted teeth.

"Home? You are home, Bryce," answers the pudgy announcer with a laugh that clinks the silver bars in his braided hair. However, the skepticism of his earlier words is gone. "You get to live another day as the King's champion, which is more than I can say for Meg'arum. Now, who do you want as next week's opponent? You can choose from anyone on this world or allow the bear-baiters to find someone."

"Bear-baiters?"

"Bear-baiters... Searchers... whatever you wish to call them."

My thoughts whirl like a roulette table, but only one name comes to mind. It plays on my tongue like the first lick of a sucker. I scan the crowd, barely able to conceal my anxiety. Mr. Paisley Tie's clean attire sticks out amongst the dirty peasants of this world like a newly minted coin. It doesn't take long to find him.

The announcer's eyes follow mine; then he interrupts with an afterthought. "Oh, and what name do you wish, Mr. Wilcox? Certainly not Bryce."

A wicked smile rises to my lips as I follow the rotund man into the crater's center. "Specialist Wilcox," I reply through the smile that's cemented on my lips. It's as though I'm on another high. The peak of my career may still lie ahead.

"Specialist Wilcox, our new champion, has selected next week's challenger," booms the man's voice. The color drains from Mr. Johnson's face as his name echoes through the cavern's enormous spires. To my surprise, cheers swell through the audience as they swarm Mr. Paisley Tie with blood-lust on their minds. I hope he survives till next week.

## Bobble-heads

Laughter filtered through the window, accompanying one faltering breeze that did little to diminish the heat wave outside. Gaven fanned himself with a random concert flyer as he melted into his computer chair.

"Damn AC. Can't we just have the repair guy come out?"

"And pay with what?" snapped Sarah from the back bedroom. "If you'd get off your butt and get a job, we wouldn't be in this mess."

"I'm trying. There isn't anything out there. I.T. jobs are a dime a dozen now."

Sarah harrumphed. "How do you know? You haven't left the house all week."

"We have internet, Sarah. Why should I step into this heat? Every day's more likely to give me a stroke than the last." Gaven peeled himself from the swivel chair and sauntered to the fridge in his briefs.

"Gaven, I ain't lucky enough for you to have a stroke," she patronized and walked into the living room. "And where the hell are your clothes?" She wadded the shirt she'd been folding and threw it his way.

He let it fall to the ground. "It's too hot to wear anything. If you weren't here, I'd be free-wheelin'."

"Gav... I just don't know what to do with you."

"You're doin' fine. Leave it be. I'll get a job when the recession clears up."

Sarah hobbled back into the room, her forefinger lodged in the back of her white nurse's shoe as she attempted to fit it over her heel.

"Gaven, if you're still here when I get off tonight, I may just turn you into a sofa. At least then you'd be useful." She succeeded in planting her dainty feet in the footwear and tugged at the bottom of her white uniform shirt. Her final words carried from the hallway. "I want you out. I just can't take it anymore."

"Love you too, Sis," Gaven shouted, flopping back into his chair before the door slammed.

"That's three times this month. Maybe this time she's serious," commented the floppy-eared bobble-head standing next to the monitor. Its robust nose and black and white spots were characteristic of a renowned cartoon.

"Nah," Gaven muttered dismissively and flicked its long, white snout. The spring retracted, sending the semi-attached head bouncing. "So what you wanna do today, Patches?"

"Ga-ave-en, yo-ou kno-ow I ha-ate tha-at. Cut it out," replied the three-inch-high, plastic caricature. Gaven belched and sat down his generic can of pop. As the momentum slowed, Patches added, "Look, you know why I'm here. Why do we have to play this game every morning?" His voice had gained a familiar tone of frustration.

"Because... it's fun," replied Gaven with a patronizing smile. "And you can't do anything about it. I put you in that doll. Now, you have to sit back and take it: a day-by-day, lifelong journey with me. That is... unless you want to tell me where Blake is?"

A slow growl echoed from the small dog, but never met his black, painted lips. "Blake is out of your reach and not part of our bargain." Patches' tone clearly showed he was trying to regain an advantage in this relationship. "You have a job to do. Find my eleven brothers before the solstice. Maybe as a boon for good service my

Mistress can come to some further arrangement with you regarding Blake."

Gaven chewed on a greasy fingernail and idly scrolled through an E-bay antiques store. "I already have five of them shipping here, so don't get your panties in a twist." With a snort he added, "Who is this mysterious Mistress anyway?"

"Also not part of our bargain. You'll find out when she arrives... assuming my brothers are all present." The growl was back in Patches' voice, but Gaven didn't seem to notice as he typed away.

"Six." He picked up the bobble-head and showed it the screen. "That is one of your brothers, right?" A small, blue, ceramic turtle was plastered on the screen from several different perspectives. A familiar, nine-pointed star was stamped into the bottom of its shell.

"Yes. You've done well."

"Thanks." With another flick of the plastic nose, Gaven dove back into his web search. Patches' undulating growl bobbed into the background. *Knock-Knock...* "Package for Gaven Jacobs!"

"One seh-cond!" he shouted. Gaven smiled at the dog figurine and flicked its nose again.

"I hate you," it said.

Gaven winked. "Just messin' with you. Be right back."

Gaven got up and went to the door, opening it a crack while keeping his bare legs hidden.

"Where do I sign, Mr.... oh, poop." Gaven added the scatological expletive because he wasn't looking at his usual delivery guy. He was, in fact, looking at a four-foot-tall bear. It was obviously fake: the kind that usually moves in jerks and stutters to bad music at restaurants where screaming kids eat cardboard pizza. Gaven might have thought it was a suit, except for the nine-pointed star branded between its comically large, too round, too blue eyes.

The only other thing Gaven noticed about the bear was its arm, which was cocked back and came shooting through the gap between the door. It smashed into his face and turned the world to stars and blackness.

As he lost consciousness, he thought, *If I bleed on the rug, Sarah's gonna kill me.*

Images danced behind Gaven's eyes as he felt himself floating above his body. A plush giraffe did the tango with a die-cast dump truck with square eyes. They stepped and twirled in the center of a circle drawn in lamb's blood, a summoner's circle taken from an ancient Jewish scroll that was clear enough to copy, but Gaven had never fully understood. Two sock monkeys pulled him in to dance while a music-box ballerina twisted in place with tears like molasses dripping over the fixed, porcelain smile on her lips.

"Time to play," a voice said. And he wanted to play. He really did. It was better than working a job he'd hated, for people he felt would have made better prison guards than call-floor managers.

But before he could step in the circle, a white shoe stepped in his way. It was tapping. Gaven followed the foot to a let, the leg to hips, and the hips to hands perched on either side. As his eyes found their way higher, they discovered his sister's shoulders and face.

"Wake up," she spat.

Gaven did just that. His shoulders were sore. The room was dark and his eyes took their time adjusting. Something bubbled behind him like stew in a pot. The smell of burnt plastic and copper permeated the air. He was also certain from the slight breeze drifting by that he was still without pants.

"Is Mr. Gaven awake?" a tinkling voice said, pulling him from what must have been a dream of Sarah. The pitch was a child's, but the command in her tone belonged to a Catholic Mother Superior.

"Where am I," Gaven croaked.

His arms suddenly hurt even more, and he became aware that he was hanging by them due to a sudden jerk. His eyes focused in the faint light, and Gaven finally made out the light drifting into the room through cracks in the planks nailed over the windows. Shadows of stuffed animals and dainty ballerinas called to him from the depths of a little girl's bedroom. But, the colors were faded; whites were now grays, pinks were the color of milk mixed with blood, and the lace and cobwebs had grown together into a single lattice. In the center of the room, a kerosene heater hissed out warmth, and an iron cauldron hung over the top of a wooden tripod. A low table, a child's table, sat next to it. Seated at it was a figure no more than four feet high. Her hair was curled, and her clothes were new. Were her fingers not tapping on the table, Gaven would have assumed her a doll.

He looked up and spotted a shelf on the wall. Patches, his Patches, was there. There were also five other figurines that he didn't recognize, but had the same distinct characteristics as the bobble head in which he'd trapped that… thing.

The bear trundled into view from behind him, stooped down, and pulled out the chair for the girl. She turned and Gaven saw her face, the sort of face that photographers put in their portfolios and that all mothers hope their daughters might resemble.

"Mr. Gaven," the girl said with a smile a piranha would envy, "it's time for my tea party. You're invited. Isn't that nice?"

"Now, little girl," Gaven replied, "I don't think you want...."

Her titter cut through his bravado like scalpels. She covered her mouth with one hand; then lowered it and said, "Did you think I was asking? Do you have any idea what it is that you're involved in now... what toys you're playing with?"

"I know things. Lots of things. I'm nobody you want to mess with."

The girl stepped closer. The bear lifted her by the waist and placed her on his shoulders. She crossed her ankles and bounced her heels on his chest, then leaned over and said, "I know a few things, too. And we're going to talk about them... over tea."

The bear approached the table, grabbed a small china cup, then filled it from the pot with a ladle. The contents dripped down in long, oily strands. A preposterous amount made its way into the cup, but did not spill.

From the shelf, the Patches bobble-head shouted, "Gaven... Don't drink it! That's not my Mistress!"

The girl shot the toy a withering look. Its small, black nose drooped down.

The bear turned and the girl riding his shoulders looked at Gaven, saying "Are we ready for our tea?"

Gaven gulped, stilling himself for what might be in the beverage. His imagination fluttered through the possibilities: poison, enchantment, mind control. What was this child up to? Not a child, he couldn't think of her that way. The Oriental slant of her eyes gave an insight into her lineage, but that wasn't what stopped him. Her grey eyes held years of knowledge, a wealth of experience, and peered into his thoughts, past his defensive, boastful façade, and into his soul. A chill slid down his spine.

"What are you gonna do with me?"

"Hmm…." She pressed her lips together and tapped an extended finger to them in thought. "What to do? I used to be a lot like you." She emphasized her point by tapping his forehead with the same finger. "But I had something more than talent. You lack training. You have potential, even skill, but your heart is mottled. You have yet to pick a side."

"What does that matter?"

The child grinned from her perch like a knowing mother. It was odd to see such a look on someone so youthful. "It makes all the difference." She grasped his chin between her thumb and forefinger, forcing his mouth open with surprising strength.

Gaven couldn't resist. He sputtered as she poured the steaming liquid down his gullet. Much of it spilt down his chin, neck, and bare chest, scalding him inside and out. When the dainty cup was empty, he gasped. Patches turned away. Evidently, even seeing his enemy suffer this treatment was difficult.

"You would turn away rather than watch your jailer drink?" asked the child without looking at Patches. "It isn't like I'm torturing him."

"You don't call that torture?"

"Not in the least, but if you would like…" Finishing the statement, the bobble-head watched as she rolled up a puffy sleeve and her fingernails grew an inch under her stare. Her motherly grin turned malicious as she stroked Gaven's chest and neck with the nails like an affectionate lover. Then, like a scorpion striking, she drove them halfway into his chest and raked deep gashes down, through his chest hair and across his ribs. Gaven screamed, but his voice was vacant, hollow. It turned to a wail, a whine, and then disappeared entirely while the young girl switched sides. Gaven's mouth remained open, his face contorted, but no sound escaped.

He tried to summon the words of a spell to mind, something that would release his bonds, but nothing came to his rescue. The pain overwhelmed all rational thought.

Patches stuffed his head beneath an arm while the other five bobble-heads lengthened their necks for a better look. "Eustes, you were always such a pansy. What's wrong with you?"

"It's too 'orrible," came Patches' muffled reply.

The turtle chuckled in a gruff voice. "He's the bastard that put me in here. I say he's gettin' what he deserves." The other toys murmured their agreement. "No one locks Demi-Gods away without paying a price."

"See, I knew we weren't so different," added the girl with a final swipe of her hand. She licked her fingers with ecstasy and motioned for the bear to lower her to the ground.

"We'll never be like you," replied a small, ornamental flamingo from amongst the group. "He deserves what he gets, but you will never be revered like us. The remaining lineage of Zeus will prevail. Our brothers will find us."

"Revered?" she asked with a grin. "You can't be serious. Your line is so diluted with mortal blood that you're hardly a match, even for this fool." She flicked her gruesome hand at Gaven, splattering his blood-streaked body. "No one even knows you exist, and you're hardly revered. I'll have the lot of you bobbing on my shelf within a day's time."

The awful creature knew more than Gaven thought possible. How? Who was she?

"Santie, your plan will fail. You must know that," replied the turtle.

The liquid began boiling inside Gaven. He tried to groan, but still no sound crossed his lips. So much for an enchantment. He had to settle things down, sooth the fire erupting inside him. Suddenly, faint shadows flew across the walls as though people were running by. He glanced around hoping for salvation, but no one else was present. The dark shapes continued to course through his vision, and the others didn't seem to notice.

A cold whisper interrupted the fire in Gaven's soul, "They all misread the prophecy." Gaven listened to the voice with agonizing anticipation. "Watch the visions she gave you. They are biased, but hold some truth."

*The shadows came into sharper focus as the apparition spoke. Before Gaven, lines of beings torn from myth and legend struggled with one another. On top of a mountain that wasn't there seconds before sat an empty throne. Gaven peered down at the battlefield and the three remaining Gods. Zeus, his blood pouring like rain on the earth below, was at the base of the mountain facing the others. Shiva stood apart, all six blades dyed crimson. Rage wafted from her like an aerial contagion. Where she stepped, disaster befell the earth. The other figure was unfamiliar to Gaven; a woman of tall, thin stature, dressed entirely in leathers. Cold radiated off her as fast and ominously as the others. Where she stood, icebergs formed and glaciers grew.*

*"His blood is to raise an army. He protects the humans. I can only do so much to help him. Shiva is strong and her followers cruel."*

*"Who are you?" Gaven whispered.*

*Santie's head whipped around. "You shouldn't be able to speak."*

*"No time. Release their bonds, and I will find you on the other side." With that the chill in his ear spread, banishing the poison as though it never existed.*

Gaven fell to the floor with a grin. "Olly Olly Oxen Free!"

The girl shrieked like she'd spotted a mouse. She cried, "Fuzzy Wuzzy, Get him back on the chains!"

The bear turned its blank, button eyes toward Gaven and lurched forward. Gaven giggled, suddenly intoxicated by the absurdity of being chased by a murderous teddy bear. He scrambled to his feet, turned and ran with the thump-thump of the bear's toeless stumps pounding the floor behind him.

A boarded window stood three stories up, but it didn't matter. Gaven leaped through the hallway and high foyer, crashing through the window as though it were Styrofoam. It was dark out and, to his surprise, wasn't on ground level. He fell hard on the shingled porch roof, rolled down, and tumbled to the ground. He landed on his back with a crack.

*Crack?* Gaven thought to himself.

He wanted to ponder this further, but above him, a murderous, furry shape dove down with a precision he envied.

Gaven rolled right, avoiding the attack just in time for the bear's claws to dig into the ground. Leaping to his feet, Gaven raced down the sidewalk faster than should have been possible for his pudgy body. He sailed over a row of dead rosebushes, the bear crashing through close behind.

Gaven marveled at how effortless it was to move. So much so that he almost stepped onto a garden hoe. Skipping a step, he bent down and scooped up the shovel lying next to it. Gaven stopped, counted three luxurious breaths, then turned and swung.

The bear's head popped off neatly, the shovel's blade ringing as the stuffed orb spun through the air.

Gaven laughed and peered back at the building he'd just escaped. Forty years ago, he was sure it was the sort of house that was on the cover of magazines, but now it was a ruin.

He thought for a moment about burning it down. If he did, the six spirits he'd worked so hard to entrap would burn with that little, creepy witch. But that would mean he'd no longer have what he needed to find Blake.

He asked aloud, "Oh for Pete's sake, Gaven... she's moved on. Do you really want to die trying to find a girl you fell in love with in the third grade?"

He did. He'd learned sorcery in the hope of finding her and casting a love spell... but just to start. He'd let her go, just as soon as he knew she wouldn't leave him, that she was used to loving him enough that she wouldn't think to go elsewhere. It was still just as worth it to him as it had been when he'd signed his first pact in blood to gain the power he needed.

"Fool," the cold woman said into his ear. The world slowed, and he thought he could see his breath. The voice continued, "I once chose a husband by his feet. I thought I knew what I wanted and I got a loving husband, but not the one I'd planned. And when I realized I could not live with him, it broke his heart. Do you think you can make anyone love you?"

"No," Gaven admitted. Especially not Blake.

Gaven turned and said, "What should I do?"

The woman was there. She looked down and touched his cheek with icy fingers, stooping lower than Gaven expected to be necessary. She said, "You must decide. You could walk away. You could destroy half of the remaining real magic walking among you. Or you could finish what you started and take on the wicked creature that wounded you."

Gaven looked down at his bloody shirt. The wounds didn't hurt anymore, but he remembered the hunger, the malice in that little freak's eyes. If he could potentially have found a love lost to him for twenty years, have some chance of holding it in his sway for even a short time, then what must that witch be prepared to use the Demis for?

Gaven looked up into to the woman's clear, pale-blue eyes. "That bitch is going down."

The woman smiled. "Then go with the blessings of Skadi. May your blade bite deep."

She disappeared into a shower of frost. Gaven looked back at the house. Then, two things caught his eye. One was sticking out of a stump not far away. The other was pulling into the house's driveway.

A plan formed.

119

## Strange Circumstances

The little girl stomped back and forth. Gaven heard her through the door he'd snuck up to, which was no small feat considering what he was trying to balance under his arms. He heard her shout, "Where is that... naughty bear!"

Gaven kicked open the door with one foot and stared across the floor, eye-to-eye with the prepubescent witch.

"Your Fuzzy Wuzzy lost his head. He's currently fertilizing the garden."

She turned and replied tartly, "What's in the box, Mr. Man?"

Gaven shifted his item. "Delivery. I signed for you. I'm curious how you diverted my auctions here."

She swung her hips a little and replied, "You were hanging up there for a lot longer than you think. But that doesn't matter. I want my dollies."

"I don't know. I don't think you've been very good."

The girl's face contorted. "I... want... my... DOLLIES!"

She leapt at him, fingers curled into claws. Gaven threw the box in her way with his right hand and slipped the hatchet he'd found with his left. The girl tore the box in half, spraying the bare rose stems Gaven had packed into the air. He slid his hand along the blade, and when he felt the bite and wetness in his palm, he cried a word in Latin.

The girl's eyes grew wide. She recognized the spell just as the vines wrapped around her, rooting her in the floor.

"Told you. I know lotsa' things," Gaven added with a sense of victory.

Dozens of thorns pierced the girl, holding her in place. She screamed, "This won't hold me forever, you meanie-head!"

Gaven stepped back into the hall, gathered the six dolls, each with its small, nine-pointed star, from beside the door, and muttered, "They don't have to."

He set the dolls in a half circle on the floor and stepped toward the shelf.

The girl cried, "You can't… it's not the solstice. Are you stupid or something?"

"The solstice is just the deadline. After that, they're locked into their forms and the magician doesn't get his wish. But I don't care about the wish anymore."

Grabbing a stool, he climbed up to the shelf and gathered the remaining six figures serenaded by her screams. He ignored her threats and pleas, even the snapping of the first vine, as he arranged them in the circle.

The incantation came easily from memory. Patches looked up at him and said, "Thank you."

Gaven winked and spoke the last magic word.

Each doll cracked. Then, a figure burst from within them. They stood beautiful and majestic, amazing and impossible. Gaven looked up at them with a newfound sense of accomplishment. "I release you from your bonds. No strings."

The lanky woman who'd been an ornamental flamingo until moments ago stepped forward to strike him. A hand came out and caught the bone-splintering blow.

A very un-Patches like voice interjected, "We're even. Which is a shame, because we could have done something about his… condition."

Gaven looked down at himself and finally understood. With a shrug, he said, "Eh, I'll deal with it."

They nodded and let him pass. He didn't look back to see what they might be doing to the childish witch, but a block away, he smelled the smoke and heard the sirens from the fire trucks hurrying to the house in vain.

Sarah came through the door and kicked off her shoes, glad to be at the end of her shift. Gaven had been missing for over a week and she wanted to see if the answering machine had any messages from the cops. First, she would get a glass of wine, but only because she didn't think she could take another blank tape without some fortification.

"Hi, Sis," a small voice said.

Sarah yelped in surprise and turned. She couldn't believe her eyes. A four-foot-tall doll was standing in her floor wearing the same boxers Gaven had been wearing when she last saw him. It had deep scratches in its chest, painted red. And it was smiling.

The doll spoke. "Well, the good news is I won't be eating your food anymore. But the bad news… that's going to take some explaining."

## Demonic Supervision

James looked forlornly across the filled pews at the casket occupying the front of the room. It was closed, appropriate considering what had happened, but an enlarged picture was perched on a tripod next to the maple casket. A well-groomed man in his thirties with olive skin and thick Italian hair stared out at the darkly clad audience. The grin on his face said, 'I own you,' and to most, he'd be right.

*God, I hope this façade holds up through the funeral. Samantha won't have time to rekindle it in this crowd.* He glanced curiously to his right. The thin brunette seated next him mimicked his concern as she periodically scanned James's face. Her wide, dark sunglasses and flimsy, black hat hid her from most of the friends and family, but James watched her eyelashes flutter behind the tinted lenses and grimaced.

*You better be worth it. If it wears off, you're dead,* he swore silently. As an afterthought, he added, *assuming I last long enough. How do you kill something as old as her?*

The question faltered as paranoia crept up his spine, starting as a small tingling sensation. James glanced from family to family, relative to relative. *Greedy bastards! Wouldn't lift a hand to help me while I was alive without payment. I should take them all now, end any hope of a future.* James lifted his hand and leaned toward the pin cushion of a man who sat wheezing in front of him. He extended cold fingers toward the back of the man's neck but before they touched, Samantha slapped his hand down.

"I didn't bring you here for revenge," she hissed, tightening her matching black dress jacket with a tug.

"I know, but all it'd take is a touch," he replied in his thick, New York accent. "And they deserve it."

"So did you. Their time will come. The only reason I brought you here was to say goodbye to your kids. That's what you wanted, right? Or was that a lie?"

*Yeah, that's what I said. You wouldn't have brought me here for anything less,* thought James, but that wasn't what he said. "I know, and I do. I know they won't hear me, but I have to see Joe's speech after the sermon. He's the one in the front row, looks just like me." He pleaded with her maternal side, something long lost to someone like her, but he'd built his empire from the ground up, had sold sand to Afghans and ice to Eskimos, or so he'd told the countless reporters in his later years. Samantha turned back to the front and assessed James's son, who was dressed in a black tie and suit. He could've been the man in the picture.

The minister standing a few feet from him was praising the dead man's exploits. "A man of great importance, countenance, and conviction, James Trevis walked across this world like a giant, bowing to no one." The garbed man's tone held a bit more grit than it normally did, as though some of the words were being filtered.

"You'd think with all the money I gave this place, and the protection, the guy'd give a better sermon." The obese man in front of James turned quizzical eyes on him. His gaze glared from under a bushy, grey mantle before turning back to the sermon with a cough.

"It's hard for these pitiful excuses for missionaries to lie. Their egos reflect only their greed," Samantha replied.

"So what?" asked James, his Brooklyn accent bristling under the woman's scrutiny, "You sayin' they don't serve a God... that they can't help people find heaven?"

He'd never been much of a churchgoer and had never been saved, but the idea that none of the people that answered God's calling were pure infuriated him. When he'd died, there weren't pearly gates and angelic voices echoing through the clouds, but he understood why. There were a few dozen murders looming over his head. He'd hoped for more, paid the church a few mil when it was looking grim, asked for a prayer or two and said a few of his own: Hail Marys and such. But it hadn't helped. No surprise there. But someone somewhere had to be better, more deserving.

"No, they do, but they're all flawed," she muttered with detestation. Then, her tone took on a nostalgic, hungry undertone. "None of them have anything on Moses. Now that was a man I could savor. He actually stood for something. He was so pure, he glowed." Her eyes took on a distant glimmer.

"Sam, you're one pessimistic bitch," he assessed shaking his head.

"Wouldn't you be after a thousand years of escorting the damned, growing thinner with each age as the mortals lose sight of even attempting to live a good life? How am I supposed to live off the scraps of morality? You know what they're saying now? Heaven's where a bunch of Mormons will be sitting around a table playing Scrabble, but Hell's where the party will be. Women, sex, drugs, and renewed vigor each day, as though Hell were a lust-filled, eternal Groundhog Day where you get to be Bill Murray. It's only getting worse with kids today."

125

The feeling of paranoia flared again, and James scanned the crowd. His eyes settled on a random child sitting amongst the funeral visitors. *Who is that? I don't remember her...*

He hadn't paid much attention to people later in life, his time being consumed by running the family business, but this innocent girl's pigtails swirled, and her eyes landed on his like anvils; black, consuming orbs with a smoky swirl at their center.

*Oh God, those eyes.* He shuddered and turned his attention to another section of the church audience. A young boy, no more than eight, caught his attention, and the boy's head spun one-hundred-eighty degrees with inhuman speed. Another set of damned eyes glared at him. The paranoia quickened, tickling his spine as though he were being watched from every angle. Both children had densely fluctuating auras.

"Why do they use children?" he whispered, glancing at the floor in an attempt to quell the nauseous feeling of insects skittering in his stomach.

"They?" asked Samantha.

"Your co-workers. Doesn't seem like your magic mask is doin' much."

Her eyes narrowed and she glanced around. "I told you coming to your own funeral was a bad idea. But you had to see your kids again," she replied in a patronizing whine.

*If only you knew.*

"Time to go," Samantha said.

"Like hell," James spat back.

"That wasn't a suggestion," Samantha retorted. Her eyes were darting from one of the cursed children with dead eyes back to the other. She wrapped her fingers around James's arm and squeezed until he thought her fingers would rip into the strange flesh of his current arm.

He bit his lip. He wanted to yell at her as she jerked him up like a mother might snatch a disobedient child out of a high chair. He didn't yell. He realized there was no point in protesting.

At least he'd seen Joe's face. That would have to be enough for now.

*No matter what you say, Sam, I'm goin' to take the time I need before we cross the River.*

A few eyebrows rose as they stepped lively toward the entrance, but only a few. It was easy enough to assume they were overcome and needed fresh air, James guessed. But the quick steps Samantha took were beginning to make him wonder.

"What the hell, Sam?" James said as he tried to keep up. She hadn't let go of his arm. "You piss someone off at the office?"

"Those aren't co-workers, you idiot," she hissed, glancing back over her shoulder. "They're scavengers."

*Great, like my day could get any worse.*

James had a thought. "We're in a church. Aren't we safe or something?"

Samantha spun him around and looked him square in the eyes. She spoke through gritted teeth and said, "You half-witted sacks of water. You think because you build houses to the Most Holy that you can shut out the Accursed. You forget that though all the world is a temple, unspeakable things still walk among you. If you wish to make it to your appointed fate, then do as I say, when I say it, and do not question me. Are we clear?"

James started to protest, but then felt the hairs on the back of his neck stand on end. He knew the feeling, the same as the first time someone drew a gun on his back, the same as when Louie had smiled and shook his hand with the same fingers he'd used to write the contract he'd put on James's head. He looked out the corner of his eye, back through the open doors where his funeral was still taking place, and there they were.

The children were in the pews, one on either side of the aisle. They peered around the ends and stared at him with those dark, bottomless orbs.

James looked back at Samantha. Then, he looked back at the kids.

They'd somehow reached the doors.

"Let's go," James muttered. Samantha opened the door and they were off at a run.

As Samantha sped from the church, she tore off her dress and tossed aside her hat. The clothes ripped and fell away, and new ones took their place. She was now dressed in a pair of loose, white, cotton pants and a sleeveless, black blouse. As they rounded a corner, Samantha stopped, grabbed the lapels of James's blazer, and pulled downward, jerking off his entire suit like a magician pulls a tablecloth from under a set dinner table. A blue work shirt and pair of black jeans appeared underneath.

"Won't fool them too much, but anything is better than nothing," she said. "Now move."

He didn't have to be told twice.

"Where are we goin'?" he panted as they ran.

Samantha replied, "Your journey to your end is only just begun. But the next step on your path begins where your last living ones ended."

*Criminal always goes back to the scene of the crime,* James thought. *I just always thought it would be in my original skin.*

James looked back. In a window overlooking the street they were about to turn off of, two sets of empty eyes stared back.

They ran like sprinters. Samantha didn't seem to tire. The body she had procured for him, the shell of another unfortunate soul now no longer among the living, was working well enough despite having no pulse.

*Apparently, the walking dead don't need smoke breaks.*

Blocks turned into miles. Again, only a few people turned their heads as the pair passed by. Neither their pace, nor the cursed children who somehow moved without being seen, drew the attention of the living.

James saw the building ahead, the warehouse where a man he'd never before met put two .32 slugs into the back of his skull. He could still feel the sting of the shots and the way his stomach had rolled over when he understood that this was the end. He didn't know how he was going to step in there again without burning it down.

*Maybe that's what I'm supposed to do.*

His train of thought was cut short by an arm flung across his chest. He looked up to see Samantha staring down the deserted stretch of street.

One of the children was in the road. And he, maybe it, was smiling.

"Alley," she said. "Now!"

# Strange Circumstances

They dodged down a dead end. James's eyes darted everywhere as panic set in. Samantha said, "Get to the end. Don't try to get away unless I say, and then run like your ass is on fire and don't look back. Are we clear?"

"Yeah," James mumbled. He found a bunch of empty boxes that once held produce stacked up for the garbage man. He jumped behind them, peered over his cardboard fort, and waited.

The children stepped into the alley, one from each side of the entrance. Their mouths were now rictus grins and their teeth were rows of needles.

"Stay back, you cockroaches," demanded Sam. "He's property of All Creation now. Try to take him, and I will end you."

The children didn't say anything. Their legs extended, turning their tiny, dark suit pants into shorts and ripping the backs of one's suit and the other's dress. Claws grew from their fingers and their mouths turned to muzzles.

Samantha spat, "Damn… why doesn't that ever work?"

She let one foot fall back. The small terrors ahead hunched over and loped into a sprint. James swallowed hard. *How can I both be dead and nervous?*

From between Samantha's ring and middle finger, on her right hand, a long, curved blade split the skin. It flashed in the dim light as the gleaming inner edge of the blade's curve split the first child's head from his shoulders.

The other screamed and dove forward, claws first. The fight turned frantic and gruesome. The blade nicked flesh, tore through muscle, and hewed bone in two. Teeth and claws did no less damage, though, and Samantha's pale pants were soon stained arterial crimson.

Still, she was the better of the two. Soon, the little girl's head fell next to the first.

Samantha let the blade retract into her arm. She held her side, leaned up against the wall, and called back to James, saying, "It's okay. Come out."

There was no answer. She stumbled to where he'd hidden himself and found no one, only an empty space next to a door to the back of a restaurant. She hadn't seen it before, behind the crates.

Two blocks away, James panted as he ran. "One look, kids. One look while they put my ass in the ground. Then send me to Hell, Jersey, or wherever else, but let me see you one last time."

The hiss from behind him ran through his soul. "We are your children, your true children."

James tripped and rolled to an undignified heap in the road. Six sets of empty eyes stared out at him from a loose circle of child-like bodies. He laughed nervously. "I only had two kids, not half a dozen."

"No, you sired six, and none survived." The children closed the circle by a step. In James's mind flashed a girl he knew from school. He had lost his virginity in her warmth, but she'd moved away a few weeks later. He then saw a basket with a baby in it. A note addressed to him was attached, claiming the child was his.

"That wasn't mine."

One of the demons grinned. "You are my father. I died in an orphanage from abuse. You put me there." The children closed the circle by another step.

James's mind went to college. At a frat party, sophomore year, a girl was wasted but willing. He saw her at a couple more parties that semester, but she dropped out of school before the year's end. A little girl is born, and grows before his eyes into a familiar figure. She knocks on the door of his father's home and is turned away. Hungry and cold, she turns to the street and is forced to sell her body. James is her first buyer. Nine months later, another daughter comes into the world. James can't have his wife finding out about the hooker, so he buries both of them in a cemetery, still alive.

"I came to New York looking for my father. You paid your own sixteen-year-old daughter for sex, and then buried her alive with the granddaughter you also sired."

James stammered, "That's impossible. I would know. Neither were my kids, she was just a hooker after my money."

"Just like the other three?" Their voices raised in an eerie chorus as the circle closed by another step. Three more hookers… three more hookers, and three more shallow graves tumbled through his brain.

James straightened, "This must be a trick. You can't tell me that not a one of those whores was lying."

"One of your whores lied." Another step, another vision… This time, of the housekeeper. She was an illegal immigrant, so when she got pregnant and came to James, he asked if it was his. She said no. She had seen at least one of the hookers, and didn't want her own hole in the ground. "You had her deported. She had no money for proper health care. She and the baby died in childbirth."

James actually shed a tear. "That wasn't my fault." He wiped his eyes. "But I know you're lying little imps. What of my living children? You said I sired six and none lived. My boy Joe looks just like me."

"No, Joe looks like your father. Your brother always looked more like him than you did. He spent a lot of time with Julie, far more than you." Another step, the ring of children was almost touching him. A montage of his wife and brother betraying his trust in a carnal act flooded his mind over and over again.

A splash of acrid, black blood shocked him back to reality. Sam, blade gleaming in the afternoon sun, stood above in a portrait of fury. "I told you not to run." James flinched with shame. The calm voice was so much more painful than her screaming would have been. "They nearly took you. I haven't lost a contract in ten thousand years, and you practically hand yourself to them."

"You said, if I paid attention in death, I might learn something about my life. I have." James's whisper was almost inaudible. "I release you from your contract. It's time I took my place in Hell." The circle of blood around him opened into a pit and James vanished below.

## Laundromat

Ned stepped into the Laundromat an hour after he'd left it, trusting that no one would want to steal his underwear, socks, and other dilapidated articles of clothing from the washers. He'd used the time get a bite to eat and some more quarters. Now, he was back to get things into the dryers so that he could finish up the weekly chore and get back to his apartment in time to catch Letterman.

The Laundromat was at its usual level of activity on a Tuesday evening, which is to say all but deserted. In addition to Ned, there was one other patron: a balding fellow wearing a threadbare wife-beater under a flannel shirt that looked like it had seen better days. It barely covered the man's belly, something that appeared to have had more than a few beers in its time.

The guy in flannel was sipping on a Styrofoam cup big enough to stuff your fist into and kept his eyes on a copy of *Entertainment Weekly*, skillfully held in one hand. He had a set of earbuds in, though Ned couldn't track them back to any obvious sound device. Ned wasn't sure if he'd ever seen the guy before or not, but he wasn't looking for conversation, and the guy in flannel didn't seem in the mood to give any.

Ned ignored him and went about getting his laundry switched over. As he twisted the knob on the last one, dropping quarters into the belly of the device and getting his mixed colors rotating toward dryness, he noticed that one of the guy's dryers was open. The clothes inside were in danger of spilling onto the floor.

Ned looked at the timer on the dryer and saw that it had a good twenty minutes left and, being the sort of person who believes in

Laundromat solidarity, he stepped over to the man to inform him of this. Just tucking another man's clothes back into a machine without letting him know seemed a bit rude.

Ned came up on the man's left side, but the guy showed no sign of recognizing anyone entering his personal space.

Ned said, "Hey, buddy…"

The guy still didn't acknowledge him.

Ned reached out, hesitantly, and tapped the gentleman's flannel shoulder.

"AHHH!" the man cried. *Entertainment Weekly* flew into the air. So did the cup. When they came down, the magazine landed first and the cup burst open, sending a thick, red spray all over the open pages.

"Jeez," Ned said, "I'm sorry!"

"Crap," the flannel stranger muttered. "You scared the living piss out of me."

"I said I'm sorry," Ned protested. "I was just trying to tell you about… about your…"

The man was rooting around in a basket of dirty-looking clothes for something absorbent as Ned stuttered. The man said, "Spit it out, will ya?"

But Ned was having a problem "spitting it out". He was now transfixed by the fluid that had spilled from the cup. The contents were, as mentioned before, thick and red… sticky, even. And Ned knew, as much as he didn't want to, exactly what they were.

"That's blood."

The other man stopped for a second. "I hope not. I ordered a cherry slushy."

Ned shook his head. "I've seen enough blood to know blood, and that's blood, dammit."

The stranger found a towel that still moved like cloth, as opposed to the number of crunchier ones in his basket. Taking it in hand, he stooped and began mopping the spill. "Look buddy, just ignore it," he grunted.

"What the hell are you, some kind of vampire?" Ned asked, disgusted.

The man stopped, took a deep breath, and peered up at Ned with an expression of frustration and defeat.

"My god," Ned hissed. "You are a vampire."

The man went back to cleaning. "Okay, you got me. I'm a vampire. A Nosferatu. A creature of the night. Bleh, bleh. What are you going to do, Tweet about it?"

"Oh, my god." Unfortunately, he couldn't think of anything more to say.

"You mentioned him already," the man replied.

"But...," Ned started. Unable to think of anything more insightful, he spat, "You're in a Laundromat."

"So I am."

"What the hell is a vampire doing laundry for?" Ned's eyebrows emphasized his astonishment as they reached for the heavens.

The vampire finished mopping the worst of the spill, then took the towel, cup, and book and threw them all in his basket. "Despite what you see in the movies, once they put the bite on you, you don't immediately grow a gaggle of servants. I can barely pay for my dry cleaning twice a month. How the hell am I going to afford someone to do my tighty-whities?"

Ned hopped onto one of the many laundry-folding tables and stammered, "I-I-I guess I just assumed."

"You and everyone else," the man mumbled. "I blame Anne Rice."

"You're taking this all really well," Ned said from on-high. "Either you're about to kill me and you're really good at hiding it, or you really don't care that I just figured out you're a... well..."

"You just said it ten seconds ago," the guy interrupted. "What's the problem now?"

"Had a chance to think about it, I guess," Ned replied.

The vampire sat up on the table opposite Ned. "Look. I ain't gonna kill ya. Besides, who you gonna tell?"

"I guess nobody. No one would believe me."

"Egg-zact-ly," the man said, pronouncing each syllable.

Ned looked at the security camera in the corner. He doubted it was real or hooked up to anything, but he looked back at the other man and asked, "Do you not show up on cameras or something?"

"Look pal," the man answered, "being on a liquid diet doesn't let me break the laws of physics. Being a vampire means I just need to keep a lot of bendy straws around and that I get a lot more use out of lifetime subscriptions than most, okay?"

Ned's shoulders slumped. He hadn't realized he'd been so tense, but the stranger's brutal honesty was somehow comforting. "Man, never thought of it like that. This is so weird... a vampire... in my Laundromat."

The guy leaned forward and extended a hand. "Call me Quincy."

Ned took the hand and shook it, replying with his own. "Sorry to startle you. Hey, your dryer came open."

"Aw," Quincy said as he looked over. "That's just great."

He hopped down and fixed the situation, then came back.

"I'm sorry I made you spill... dinner, I guess. I'd offer to buy you another one except, well...."

"Don't mention it," Quincy said. "It's pigs' blood, anyways. I can get more."

"That's big of you."

"I don't sweat the small stuff. Speaking of taking this well, most people are looking for the nearest pointy, wooden thing when they figure out someone is undead. You seem to be acclimating pretty quick."

"Well, it was kind of a shock," Ned replied. "But... I'm not exactly normal myself, y'see."

Quincy raised one bushy, black eyebrow. "Really? How so?"

Ned hesitated, then shrugged. "Well, it's not like you're going to run off and tell anyone."

"You got that right, sweetheart."

Ned quirked an eye at the paunchy man, and Quincy let out a hearty laugh.

"Sweetheart?" A shiver ran down Ned's spine. Just when he didn't think it could get any weirder, it did. He gave the middle-aged man an awkward smile. "Don't tell me you're a homosexual vampire with a pig fetish?" He'd intended the question to be funny, but the sarcasm never made it to his voice.

Quincy rocked the table with the next boisterous laugh, and the thin, metal legs threatened to give way. Then he composed himself in a millisecond and asked in all seriousness, "You gotta a problem with that? You're fine with me being a vamp, but when it comes to homos, that just ain't allowed."

Ned glimpsed Quincy's subtle fangs in the verbal barrage and fended him off with two palms hoisted in the air. "Nah, it's not that. I just thought you being a vamp was a big enough shock. The other thing was just the last straw." As Quincy calmed down, his shoulders slumped back to their casual resting place, and Ned let out a fearful breath.

"It ain't like that, kid. I'm just messin'. So what is this secret you don't want people knowing?"

The echo of clothes tumbling in the machines around them lengthened the silence following the question. Finally, Ned drew his eyes from the floor and met Quincy's curious gaze. "There's a reason I've seen so much blood... I've seen lots of it in my lifetime. I even dream of it, wishing it could be my blood trickling down a sewer grate or some such. It never is. I'm cursed."

Quincy laughed again, but when he saw the somber look on Ned's face, his laughter turned to a hiccough. "Wait... what do you mean, cursed? If you want to die that bad, go ahead and slit your wrists. Dying ain't so bad, but you might not want to see what's on the other side. I never made it there, but I hear it's pretty awful."

Ned shook his head. "You don't understand." He pulled up the cuffs of his long-sleeved T-shirt, exposing the scars crisscrossing the undersides of his arms. "It does no good."

Quincy's glance was curious, then widened from what had to be fear: fear of the possibilities, Ned guessed. He unconsciously pulled the sleeves of his shirt back down. "I'm cursed… and in more ways than one. How old would you say I am?"

Quincy's wide eyes relaxed as he gauged Ned. "Gotta be about twenty-three."

Ned shook his head. "I was born February 29th, 1868. So really, I'm thirty-four if you just count the leap years and one hundred forty-three if you count every year."

This time, Quincy found himself shaking his head. "So, what did you do to get this special treatment from God-Almighty himself? Or did you sell your soul to the devil? From your reaction to me, I don't think we have that in common."

"Nope, not in the least, and I'm surprised I've never met a vampire before now."

"Oh, I'm sure you have. We're around, but we don't wear big, red signs that say 'Will work for blood' or anything. At least, most of us don't." Before Ned could ask what he meant, Quincy prompted him again.

"Like I said, I'm cursed. I can't die. Every time I take a razor to my wrist, I wake up the next day, in the tub or wherever I was, with a massive headache and scabs covering my arms. It's like I can't run out of the red stuff."

The mention of an endless supply of blood brought a glint to Quincy's eyes. Ned flinched. "Sorry, the idea's just so appetizing," muttered the balding man. "You sure you wouldn't want to be a feeding trough for vampires? I mean, the benefits are great. With your unusual ability, you might not even be susceptible to the taint of feeding vamps."

The question came across in jest, but Ned could tell there was truth hidden below the surface.

"We'd make a great pair," Quincy continued. "I'm drinkin' pigs' blood because I don't wanna upset the populace, and I'm not too fond of killing people. But you pose some interesting possibilities."

"To you and every other vampire, I'm sure," Ned added. "But don't get too fond of the idea until you hear the rest. Living forever could be great, but it isn't my blood I dream about. It's the blood of all the people around me. Like you, I'm not fond of killing, either. But people that stick around me always wind up dead. It's the curse, and they don't go peacefully either. Imagine the timer on death starting early for anyone I come in contact with."

Quincy's brows knit together. "How long does it take?"

"It varies," Ned replied with a shrug. "Normally, less than half an hour."

"Sounds like a curse on others." Quincy nonchalantly checked his watch, then peered at the timer on his clothes. Finally, he turned back to Ned, weighing the risk.

"Yeah, but I always live through it. Years and years... the blood of hundreds of people flows through my dreams. And none of it's mine."

Quincy's dryer buzzed in the awkward silence and both men jumped. "It's just the dryer." Quincy laughed and tried to mask the nervous tremble in his voice by retreating to his belongings. "I can't believe that got us both." As he walked back to the table, they both heard something sizzle in one of the other dryers. Quincy turned in time to see a spark and an explosion of clothing; his preternatural reflexes barely allowing him to dodge the dryer's glass door. Ned wasn't so lucky and took the circular door in the temple. As Ned fell to the floor, Quincy's piercing scream echoed throughout the Laundromat and beyond its windowed walls. Blood sprouted from a wound on his head. Soaked hair and splintered bone tumbled down his shoulders as the injury Ned suffered transferred to the nearest person: Quincy.

In a pain-filled panic, Quincy's instincts took over. He dove for Ned, sinking his fangs into the man's cursed flesh. As Ned's cursed life's-blood flowed into Quincy's mouth, both men convulsed until they blacked out.

Ned awoke to the smell of burning flesh and the sun on his face, a war zone of scattered clothes littering the rubble around him. Unmanned fire trucks were parked haphazardly outside amongst the screaming people in the streets. Walking outside, Ned's feet kicked up clouds of greasy ash from the ground. A quick look around showed car wrecks and more ash coating everything within view. People sped from the Laundromat's vicinity as fast as they could. Somehow, the thought of people running from him made sense after all these years. He leaned against the apartment building next door and cursed as he bit into his tongue. Running his bloody tongue along his teeth, two newly-formed fangs greet him.

From an apartment above, the sound of crashing objects, moans, and thrashing limbs wafted amidst the sirens. Stepping away from the wall, Ned craned his neck for a better view. A young girl stood inside clawing at her face, her own fangs tearing into the back of her hands. Ned felt the warmth of the sun's rays on his cheeks as he stepped into the daylight, but he watched her burst into flame at that very moment.

"Oh shit! The curse!" His head reeled at the epiphany. People were turning into vampires just by being near him. Although the girl had been in the shade of the room, his curse killed her as soon as his Nosferatu ass bumbled into the sunlight.

"Is this how you want it, God?" Ned screamed at the darkening clouds above. "You wanna use me? Am I your judgment?" Something inside Ned snapped in that moment. A subtle grin crested his face, and he began loping down the street, picking up speed and running down people as they fled. "Maybe once they're all dead, God will let me rest," he muttered, followed by a maniacal laugh.

As the scourge that Ned had become slowly walked the Earth, the populace burned.

# Part Two - Flash Fiction 3x33s

While all three of us wrote a portion of each 3x33, the idea for them came from the oddly extravegant mind of David Chrisley, the self-proclaimed storyteller of our group of writers. Marshall J. Stephens and I can often be found at the computer or recording notes into an audio recorder or cell phone. David, however, spins his tales at whatever hour they come to him, often engrossing his friends, and even strangers, in stories one can only hope are figments of his imagination. When prompted, he can often be heard screaming, "I can't write the stories. They play out in my head, off my tongue, and are gone, never to be heard again."

We are thankful to his fiancée, Amanda, or whosoever conspired to restrain the man in front of a keyboard and convince him to peck his thoughts onto a digital page for a time. His contributions are forever unmatched.

## Cold

It was cold. The rain, her eyes, the gun in Trent's pocket, all frozen in place by what had to be done. He brought it on himself. Best that it be done quickly.

Shane closed the distance. "I'm sorry. I didn't know he was your brother." Shane delved in his pocket. A chain emerged with the teardrop half of a yin-yang. Stamped in front, was 'Samantha'.

Trent recognized it, identical to the one in his pocket. He would lay money the corpse on the floor had one, too.

"That bitch," Shane said.

As sirens approached, he had to agree.

## Shroud

The crimson silk parts to reveal the object of Jesse's desire-- long, smooth, and pale--stretching from where it lies, partially shrouded to a world of infinite possibility. Trembling, he reaches for it. The bone cane is fragile beneath his fingertips, its joints calcified as though formed naturally. The end arches under his hand as Jesse lifts it from the floor.

"You there!" commands a voice. "You need to put that back, right the hell now!"

Jesse turns slowly to face the museum's security guard.

"No, I don't. Ask my friends."

The mounted dinosaur skeletons all stomp in agreement.

## Flicker

Jerold looked up from his book. The words ceased making sense hours ago, but still he read on, as instructed. The wax had disappeared from the candle, yet the flame persisted... flickering... hungry.

But it didn't die. Rather, it sprang into a blazing jet of blue and took on the shape of a man.

"Why have you summoned me forth?" it... he asked.

"To right a wrong," Jerold murmured regretfully. "Kill Felix. His rule ends now."

The flickering figure nodded and dimmed. Jerold's brother would never know his adversary, but it was the only way to end the curse.

## Match

"If I let go of the match, we die."

"If you don't, everyone dies."

The match is half consumed. I still can't make up my mind.

"It's been good, hasn't it?"

"The best."

"Then, let go." His voice was just a whisper, but echoed off the cavern walls like liquid baritone.

"But your family. How will they know?"

"If the sky falls, they'll know we failed."

The match falls and fizzles in the liquid.

A speaker crackles. "You were chosen to survive. Provisions are stored in the back. Sorry to have lied to you. We love you both."

*BOOM!*

146

### Fragile

"You'll never find them," she says, clutching the Polaroid in her trembling hand. "They are out of your reach forever."

"Oh, Denise," he replies, caressing his tumbler of scotch. "You make me laugh. My guy took that photo less than an hour ago. I believe you call him Husband."

Jared stands and glides toward Denise, "But, you do have something that I want."

"You conniving bastard!"

To her astonishment, Jared plucks two vials from between her plump breasts. "Thanks, but you're no longer necessary."

"No, you can't... I need..."

Before she finishes, Jared crushes the vaccines under his boot heel.

### Recoil

I don't know which is more jarring: the force of the shotgun going off in my hands, the boom of the muzzle, or the knowledge that it won't save me.

Don't pause. Reload.

I just have to keep telling myself, "They aren't my friends anymore." The mantra starts in my head but tumbles out my lips.

From behind, a lilting voice says, "Not even me?"

"Especially you." I level my trembling shotgun on the traitor and spot the mouth of her .357. Everything slows.

"Too late," she spits.

I shudder at the explosion. Blood smears my vision... then emptiness follows.

## Traditions

Flowers sprout throughout the valley. The lake fills, echoing like waterfalls. A satyr stands beneath Delsyn's extended hand, young horns poking between fingers. The other hand holds a knife under its beard shamefully. Abomination, they call him. He is my son, and born of their rituals. The new Gods would have stopped this already. Of course, they too call him monster. The blade turns. "Sorry, Bilgas."

The satyr says, "No need, Father. I am my mother's son."

A stinger appears as Bilgas's tail extends. Delsyn's stomach splits like a baked apple under a fork.

And a village soon burned.

## Flush

Water swirls all about. The enormity of the basin my head is in when I wake is unfathomable. My legs throb from their bonds, while the blood in my skull pounds in rhythm.

"She still kickin'?" asks a woman's distorted voice from above.

"Nah." He grips the back of my neck tighter, shoving me deeper. "She quit after I got my jollies. She's got nothing left."

I breathe in deeply, but don't choke. I lose my legs; the grip weakens. I hold my head up, singing a terrible song.

They fall, ears bleeding. This mermaid has fight left, in plenty.

## Cog

"How much for the watch?"

"Whatcha got?"

"I'll give you twenty bucks."

"That's not what I asked."

"Look, I want it. What will you take for it?"

"Time. You have to give it time."

"Give it time? What are you talkin' about?"

"You reek of smoke, and your stained shirt tells me you like fast food. You're giving it away already. You won't miss another five years."

"You're crazy, but if all you want is time… sure, five years."

Sam slides on the watch, the hands spin, and Sam dies.

"You can work off the rest in the next life."

## Company

"If you make me wreck, you better hope you die," shouted Megan as her marshmallow Neon wound through the mountain curves.

Daniel quirked an eyebrow in mock surprise. "Who, me? I would never…" Despite the protest, his hand left her thigh and went to his cigarettes. Time to smoke the special cig that Witch sold him. Light… Drag… Magic words… "Sorry, I just love your curves."

As he puffed out perfumed smoke, the radio went to fuzz. Over the crackling, a voice, sultry but metallic, said, "The feeling's mutual."

Megan's door opened, dropping her on asphalt.

"Now we're alone."

## Karma

The curved blade slurps sickeningly as it's pulled free of its bodily sheath. The sound vibrates through me. I shudder.

My blade gleams in the morning light, silver... clean. *How did I miss?*

He pulls his hand aside to display the wound, there but unbleeding. I've brought the wrong tools, apparently.

The bookcase opens and reveals Dr. Weiss, wearing a mocking smile.

"Do you like him?"

I spit. "Homunculus... Nightmare made flesh... He's almost as despicable as you are."

Weiss' smile doesn't slip, "But he's for you. You asked for your brother back. Now pay me or join him."

## Sainthood

Able rummaged through his dresser. The shard had to be here.

The entryway door slammed. "Brother, what are you doing?" echoed a deep voice. "The council's tired of waiting."

Able froze in fear.

"I've just misplaced my glasses," he lied. "I'll only be a moment."

"Are you sure," the deacon replied, "you weren't looking for this?"

Able turned, terrified to see the shard in another's hands.

"Let's go see if it fits." The Priest turned toward the Stone Chamber. "Brother Abel claims he's been chosen."

Able's hand shook. He slid the shard home in his chest. "No living Saints."

## Makeover

"This is so much easier when they're dead," Angie said to me before blowing on the still- tacky nail polish. Looking at the girl, limp and peaceful like that, I had to agree.

Lighting the welding torch, I folded the thin sheet-metal around her dark-skinned arm and soldered the edges together. The hair on her clammy forearm sizzled, permeating the air as each limb was encased.

"Are you sure you can revive her?" I mused, finishing the last weld.

"She wanted a toned, bronzed body. She knew the risks." Angie opened the roof to the storm. "Raise the slab."

## Night-Terrors

The webbed wings blocked out the moon as the creature landed. It peered down its snout at Noren.

"Why disturb this sacred place?" asked the monster, smoky, green eyes churning with the question.

Noren held up one shaky hand, obviously not confident in the power of the piece of paper he held. "The producers need to talk to you, to discuss a clause in the contract."

"That clause is perfectly clear. They get their opus, and I eat them after. Run... tell them before I decide I'm hungry now. The FX Wizard did not include flunkies for protection. Go!"

## Author's Note:

Dear Reader,

Thank you for reading our first short story anthology, *Strange Circumstances*. I hope you've enjoyed reading the assorted stories we created. Check out my upcoming sequel to *Invisible Dawn* in the Altered Realities Series, *Salvation*, due out in late 2012, and Marshall J. Stephens' *Even the Dead May Die*, to be published in the near future. I certainly hope they are to your liking. Until then, look for our other novels at most online retailers.

*Weston Kincade*

## About the Authors:

Photo Courtesy of Steven Mays Photography

Creative writing has always been a passion for Weston Kincade. He's helped invest in future writers for years while teaching English. He is also the primary editor for WAKE Editing. In his spare time he writes poetry, short stories, and is working on the sequel to his debut novel, *Invisible Dawn: Book One of Altered Realities*. As the wordsmithing process continues, Weston enjoys finding great ideas in the oddities of mundane life and loves stretching the boundaries of human understanding.

To find information about upcoming books, visit me at:

Blog: http://www.authorwakincade.blogspot.com/

Facebook: http://www.facebook.com/pages/Weston-Kincade/234714006555362

Goodreads: http://www.goodreads.com/user/show/5127620-weston-kincade

Marshall J. Stephens started his first novel in 8th grade and has written stories in a variety of genres all of his life. He was born in South Carolina and now lives in Virginia with his wife and two cats. He's available for children's parties and will not be undersold. You can find more information and upcoming publications from him at http://www.marshallmakesmedia.com.

Strange Circumstances

David Chrisley lives in many places. His body may reside in the comfort of Appalachia's New River Valley, but his mind is rarely there. In his mental wanderings, he has become a student of life and a porchswing philosopher. He enjoys relating his imagined travels to anyone who will listen.

# *A Life of Death*

A paranormal coming-of-age mystery about one boy's pain and hardship endured in a small Virginia town.

Losing a father and growing up with an abusive, drunk replacement is hard enough, but when you hardly knew the first because of his constant military deployment, it alters your perspective. As a seventeen-year-old high school senior, Alex Drummond learns the value of family and the meaning of dedication the hard way, but reliving people's horrendous murders does have its upside. Join him as he struggles to find his destiny, understand love, and discover what really happened to his father and the skeletons hiding within his small home town.

**Available Now**

Printed in Great Britain
by Amazon

46897544R00090